TALES FROM THE WOODS

Tales from the Woods

Short Stories

by

DONNY BARILLA

Adelaide Books
New York / Lisbon
2021

TALES FROM THE WOODS
Short Stories
By Donny Barilla

Copyright © by Donny Barilla
Cover design © 2021 Adelaide Books

Published by Adelaide Books, New York / Lisbon
adelaidebooks.org

Editor-in-Chief
Stevan V. Nikolic

All rights reserved. No part of this book may be reproduced in any manner whatsoever without written permission from the author except in the case of brief quotations embodied in critical articles and reviews.

For any information, please address Adelaide Books
at info@adelaidebooks.org
or write to:
Adelaide Books
244 Fifth Ave. Suite D27
New York, NY, 10001

ISBN: 978-1-954351-43-1

Printed in the United States of America

Contents

The Young Boy of the Woods and the Witch

Once, long ago, my name, 'The Young Boy of the Woods' would answer so many questions. I spent my childhood, my time and my life growing up in and discovering the wilderness, every inch and every particle. I had a love of the bud, sprouting on the sweet, tender trees which blossomed every Spring. The smack of the gushing Summer rains caressed me and everything which softened upon the wild rains. As the leaves fell and swooned upon the Autumn floor, my full body, limbs and spinning head rested and slept upon the October nest which tossed every element of aroma and musky fragrance. I gently carved my way upon the white snow beds and ices of Winter's wrath. From here I deserted the trimmings of the woods and tucked for a long rest in the safety of my thick wooden cabin.

When the weather permits, I tangled through the gushing coolness of the mountain creek, which had tumbled and rolled down to the valleys and wide spread of the dew patted Spring meadow. I gathered chestnuts and stored them in my broad wooden cabin, holding them for the hunger of Winter. My garden fed me as well as many creatures of the surrounding forest; these creatures were hungry and desperate. I looked upon them as friends. Into the thicket of the splashing Autumn rain, I bathed and looked upon the sauced covering of the surrounding forest.

I would tell you of my adulthood, but in these stories, it has not yet come to pass.

Well spread, a lightly wooded forest, once motioned through the soft, gentle winds which grappling the leaves swiftly to the ground where the sky opened and the branches spoke; I trembled in the cool Autumn breath. The wooded trail, covered in black mulch and a fine spread of cedar chips, aromas of the tender seduction of nearby pastures and moonlit leaves, the sweet gesture awoke as the pause of every wind, flooded the height of the mountain north and suckled every peak. The fragrance drifted to the ground and settled as film from the nearby pond which reached softly and spirited a regal green. Gently, I fell asleep upon the base of the willow tree and traveled my way through the treasures of moaning dreams.

In the lap of the arms of the Madam of dreams, I wandered and absorbed every dash of the trickling creek. I drank as the wind buckled through me and tenderly, I tasted the sap and syrups of the heavy maple tree which loosened every leaf between the north forest to the thinning woods of the south.

To the east spread the fields of wheat. As I waded thick through the grains of the hook and the curve of her thighs, my breath resumed a perfect flood of trembling flesh which filled each pocket and museum of my lungs. Walking tenderly through the flood of me, I tickled and rose full of laughter as the sweet cloak of the ink black sky motioned upon the groove of her sweet groin stretched in tapestries which sauntered from the moonlit swabbing the sky.

I reached the majestic oak tree. She rattled her heavy branches and loosened a bushel of leaves across my shoulders and slowly, I walked through the mumbling mound of slivers of parchment which crinkled beneath my feet.

"Please sit upon the soft earth which surrounds me and lean your neck and back along my trunk. The wind ceased and will not return unless you help me and the stillness of the vast, roaming fields of wheat. The wheat feeds the farmers and reaches the mouths from far beyond the great valley, between the joust of the peaks which puncture the sky. I ask of you to defeat the dark black witch whom has placed a spell upon the fields. Climb my branches and reach the highest leaf. This leaf holds as my highest and most magical leaf. When you find her upon the high peak of the northern mountain, you must trick her into eating the leaf. This will return the winds to the soon trembling fields of wheat." said the Majestic oak.

I sat for a long, shivering entertainments of thoughts and possible edgings of plans and strategy.

"As always, I serve you madam and follow your command. I will climb your trunk and retrieve the perfect leaf." said the boy of the woods. Motioning my eyes, looking upon the reach of the branches, I stood and began climbing to the top level of the top leaf.

After plucking the highest leaf from the highest branch, I stood in the dimming light of day and looked so closely to the oak leaf, I felt the veins as they wove and interpassed. My heart began to race as I could feel the veins move and flush energy throughout itself. The veins which slipped along the edges and fullness of the leaf seemed to boast the colors green and yellow. I held the magical leaf to my ears and heard the most remote and faintest whisper. Making out no sound, rather, I felt a reunion between me and the land I am to save and love.

Needing to prepare for the journey ahead, I placed the leaf in my front right pocket and quickly motion my way to the wild mountainscape. I swiftly returned to the farthest section of the depth of the sweet, yet wild woods. Here rests the humble cabin in which I live. I packed a satchel in which I placed apples, two loaves of bread, spicy jerky and a batch of shortbread. I filled a decanter with wine and grabbed my favorite hiking stick and tuck tender beneath a cloak. My boots well suited my feet and lightened my every step. I brought my bamboo fishing pole and my tackle and net in case of a breath of free time.

I faced north and went my way. The earth lay soft and the rocks sat spread with fine moss and the leaves which rest in abundance spoke beneath my feet. I walked knee deep in the grip of morning and smiled upon the crisp light which overturned the shadow of night.

The air stood stale as the wind crept in a fast and far distance. Every breath tasted of caverns and old withered trees. By nighttime, I scheduled my path to reach the mountain pass which would levee my feet upon the rising trail.

By the edges of the night, I had an idea. Sitting by the trickling waters of the mountain's creek, I paused, drank and I thought of the black evil witch and wondered how to get her to eat the leaf. Perhaps, baked in a cake. Do witches even eat cake? With strength, I would pin her down and force her to eat it. No, not when witches have spells. Then I thought, I would pulverize the leaf into dust and place the dust in the carafe of wine. Surely, no witch could resist a fine bottle of wine.

Steeper and steeper, the path wound across the mountain as I struggled to make it just a bit higher. The sun had just recently cut across the surface of the full width of the horizon. Weeds stretching along the edges of the path coated and struck with the translucent pearl dew, quivered and soaked upon my feet.

As I hiked the steep reaching path of the northern mountain, I felt the comfort of breath and I started to breathe a bit easier. The loafing wind stretched higher and higher as the glistening shine of morning and the morning sun cast arrows of the sun upon me. As my breath resumed a normal swallow of chest and lungs, I jumped in shock and witnessed the witch, both evil and dark.

I attempted an honest smile and uttered, "Hello, who might you be? I am 'The Young Boy of the Woods'. You look tired my young lady, would you enjoy a fine mug of wine? Surely, no one could resist such a tasty treat."

She looked upon me and stood wearing a black robe with a purple rope belt. She had bizarre and mystical series of symbols on her necklaces. Her back hooked in a hump which spoke of awesome tales and stories. When I looked into her black trembling eyes, I shook and looked away to the valley of the South. Her scent, neither good nor offensive had a fragrance which remained as unique to itself. In her front belt loop, she held a hooked knife which seemed to sit so sharp, it could cleave off my head.

"Give me a gift or I will surely kill you with one of my spells. In fact, let me try this wine you have. I have a great thirst and would love the chance to quench it. Hurry before I grow bored of you, which I might already have." she said with a raspy voice.

"All I have to give is this bottle of wine. It has been well aged and tastes most delicious. Here it rests if you would kindly accept."I responded a bit more comfortably.

She suddenly fell to the earth and writhe upon it with black fluids coming out her eyes and mouth as the smoke of the morning fog began to rise off her bubbling flesh. In a fit of wild madness, she bit off the long green length of her sickening tongue. In a last blast, she gave off a sizable amount of smoke off of her deflating body.

Tenderly, the earth swelled back to the winds upon the wheat and fresh air for our lungs. The fields of wheat had returned to the wealth of there breath and sweetly I returned to the cabin, deep in the thick of the woods.

Thebis the Demon

Once, I dashed through the woods as an eagle spread upon the wind threading from the northern reach. I searched for her as the words she spoke could reach me from many miles and each throbbing passage of the breeze. The last words I heard where, "Please help. The Demon of the mausoleum has captured me in order to send you upon a hunt in trust to free him from a spell and if accomplished free me as well as save you from the spell of another fashion."

She cared for me as I cared for her. I loved her and I wanted her saved and to myself. Her name was, 'The Lady Nymph of the Mountains'. I heard no more, but I felt the trembling ache of her soon to be broken heart. She stood five foot three inches tall and held a pale complection and held a full, beautiful head of white hair. Her flesh, from her face to her feet, poised in the most perfect of manners. She walked to my cabin in the woods and must have been captured along the way. Swift, I ran to the mausoleum, willing to do whatever it took to save the life of her precious loving heart.

As I ran, the moss seemed to have grown slightly higher upon the bark of the tree. The ferns waved in the passing wind and moaned upon the scouring breath of the wind. The branches smacked and cracked against one another as the sky began to grow most humble in a patient tread of direction. The popping fall of the chestnuts gathered around me as I charged into the realm of a demon who threatened me and my tender loving nymph.

When the earth groomed old and I stood young, alive in the youth of the sweet bloom of the cherry tree and the mourning shed of the willow tree, vapors of his trembling victims of the shadow perched upon the glazes and dashing rhythms of his antiquity. Holding the fabric of my young age, I held myself in sulking posture which drove me to the blanket of the earth, soft, yet stammering upon the slices of his clever sting and temporal slashes and attacks. He roamed through the fibers of the earthly bones which shaded him to the tossing daggers which lunged at the gentle flesh. I face the now threading waters of the sky and softly I held the name 'The Demon' deeply within my ears.

Even younger, I wandered the sweet blades of the countryside which pulled moisture upon the exchange of shadow and fullness of the darkness of his stinging face. We first met in the habitat of the trembling prism of the mausoleum. I searched. I always searched, whether by meadow, by forest, mountainside or strolling creek. This day, I found the home of the dead.

He reached me dead in the picture of his face, but terrifying in the shade of his moaning sting from the eye.

Upon the slab of the granite stone and from beneath the shroud which fell upon the dusty rock of the floor, I felt the fangs of his teeth sink the verbs of mad pleasure tremble across the room. "Go to the center of the thick treasure of the woodlands and bring me the sickle of youth. If you succeed, I will free you from the misery of your soul as your love, The Nymph of the Mountains, if you fail, you will be my serf and she will die"

I looked across the mausoleum and saw her chained the the thickest wall in the room. I knew I had to save her, but first I must follow the orders of this terrifying demon.

In the full awareness of this phantom curse, I swept through the rocky, mausoleum and dashed far upon the thick green hills which led to the wealth of the forest. I was not sure if this passage took me to where I truly wanted to go but, I steamed swift across the earth and met the edge of the woods. The wild tree, vine, and branches deepened upon the moisture and mud of the pasture scouring through the patches of the resting space of the woods. With a rising wind, I heard, witnessed the scoffing voice of the demon.. Trickling through the trees, I coddled, swelled a fragrance every word which stood to drive me to terror. His body slept as a flooding erosure of a corpse trembled, his voice and phantom spirit sliced me as a fist full of blades.

I stopped on my way and deepened the trickling flavor of honey which blossomed every shade of cool stretching wind. Perhaps an hour later, I felt the summons of the thick, cool wind and gentle dash of the washing rains which caress the warm flesh of my youth and pour across me in sauces and floods. I fastened my way deeply into the covenant of relishing desire and probing youth where I would master these woods as a child and thicken the treasure of lounging ponds and fumbling creeks.

As I loosened upon these old roads, I stood wearing only a thin cloth of burlap and the eager press of these delicate shoes. I did not know what a sickle was nor the confusing use of the word "youth". I thought of the haunt of the mausoleum which brought a curse upon me, or a potential one which would fasten me as a slave. Now, Summer, the woods blossomed in a steaming hot breath. The slick steam and burning glaze spread across me in the heaviest glare of sweet smells which buckle beneath my belt and across my cropped hair which flooded in slithering sweat.

Upon the soft beds of the shaking ferns, I rested upon the shaking cloak of fastened night and pause of the welt of pounding daytime. Every dance of every quivering fern softened my eager face and freshened me to the morning chymes of a thick blooming wind.

I rose and smelled the wash of the birchwood as the wind of morning tackled across the fever of the trembling snarl of the temptation of the woods. With a current bloom of winded voices across the air, I hear the gnashing snap of teeth and the tear of the joust of terror across my tangled sweat bloomed hair. The Demon and the sting of his voice held upon me as I stammered and sauntered swiftly into the deeper edges of the wild woods.

With his raspy, frothy, blood churning voice, I spread my way into the woods. I climb the hills and deepen upon the hollow as suckling howls of the tender owls, this murder of fine black crows glamours across the bake of the sky and the warbling charms of every near by finch dashed through the branches and took to the distant edge of the mountain reach. I smiled in the flock and array as the sweet pressure of daylight fell upon me in blitzes of floods of the tender jousting birds.

Alone stood a single blackbird who took well into the air and spoke to me, "Follow me...I know the way." Frightened, I walk upon the soil and earth and held my quickest pace. Several minutes past and I lost my way into the deepest nook of this woodland grove. I spotted the blackbird and watched as he perched atop the tallest of pine trees and I took in the sweetest smell of the lavender bush which stood surrounded by the tower of the birchwood, reaching through the endless gathering of endless trees.

The blackbird sang beautiful songs and pressed her narrow beak upon the largest of rocks which slightly creased and shuddered in the dash of a crumble, so fiery I felt a surge quake in the Shadow of the trembling hub of the woods.

The blackbird opened once again and spoke of the fury of the tremble of a tender song. I looked across the hollow of these open woods and sang a song from when I reached upon the arms of my Mother and sang in rumbling breath and piercing floods.

The rock split cleverly in two and rubble released and the scythe pronounced itself as the moisture of the thickness of the woods. By handle, I gathered the blade in the grip of my hand and the flood of the hot, warming sky unfastened and released these treasures upon the moss and pebbles of the earth. As I tasted the nectar of the sweet flavor toppled from the tender voice of the screaming heaven's dome, I heard millions of whispers and thousands of screams pull me into the reach of the mausoleum, alive in the fire of the blossoming wrech.

I walked upon the threshold and deepened into the mesh of the burn of the face. In a temper, I felt my heat rise, scorch through my blood as I lunged for him with the charm of the scythe. Fire consumed the corners of the room as the blade swept the neck and spine upon the evil Demon.

I dove for the entrance and escaped with a narrow reach. In the days that passed, the woods stayed calm and the moss stays soft. The ferns blossomed and tugged upon our tender necks as the blackbird hugged close. The weather cooled and in the end, I sweetly maintained my youth.

I unfastened the chains which bound 'The Nymph of the Mountains'.

Speaking to her softly, I said, "Be at peace, you are freed from The Demon. We will walk and rejoice as we travel through the sweet scents of the heavy, wash of mint, lavender and lilacs. Please hold my hand and we will eat a feast once we reach the cabin of my in the woods."

I kissed her upon the lips and on the pale softness of her cheek. Within the cabin, we sat and warmed before the fire which removed the chill of the peculiarly cold night.

I dove for the entrance and escaped with a narrow reach. In the days that passed, the woods stayed calm and the moss stays soft. The ferns blossomed and tugged upon our tender necks as the blackbird hugged close. The weather cooled and in the end, I sweetly maintained my youth.

Lady with the Lyre

Never once have I been this far into the depths of these wild, tangled woods. The roots hooked from the soft deep soil and made their proud pronouncement, a heavy covering of weeds and the darkest shade of green which moaned with the crossing curve of wind, wrapping across the bark and tug of the canopy of leaves. I look to the sliver, gape in the rooftops of branches and tender brushing wave of the buds and eager pods. I witnessed the spread and crawl of the purple and navy bloom in the evening sky. With moments in a dash, the darkness of night posed and dredged across me as a shroud, softly. Reaching the pour and gush of the forest creek, I drank the sweetest mountain water which spread deep and hosted endless minerals and enriched rocks. Tender, a cool splash of perfect wind coiled and caressed the pale skin of my body as I walked deeper into the majesty of the emerald woods.

I stood by the arching trees, standing and towering as a tender gateway to another realm. As I walked through, scents and aromas swabbed upon me. I smelled lavender and sweet sap from the pines. Passing the tiger lily, I stopped and tucked a petal deeply in the reach of my pouch. The further charm and seduction of the scent of sandalwood pressed well into the gap of my lungs. The rosebush clung swift against my pants and the sweet smell coddled across me in the softest the most tender of touch and bloom. Further, I walked into the wild reaches of the fertile and lusty woods as quickly, I heard the beautiful, sweet sound of a perfectly played lyre and each soft note floated through the air and softly I bathed in it's moaning touch. Feeling starved for a warm touch and flooding press of dancing flesh which glazed across me, I followed the song and grew eager to rejoice with the player and the lyre.

As I approached, I heard the lyre, born of sweet magical sounds and flavors of every flower, tree, plant and bush, pull me closer and chisel through the loafing tender grace of the breath of the wind. Stepping forward, I smelled the sweet lofting fragrance of a woman. She sang of soft vocals as the humming breath of her throat and tongue and mouth gingerly found me. I turned the corner of the forest path. Her hair blossomed the color of walnut's as the spread and reach fell to the middle of her back. Her shoulders and neck halted in regal poise as her skin stayed pale. The breads of her breasts spoke of fullness and stood proud upon the freshness of the smacking wind which brought christening scents of the edge of Autumn.

She looked upon me with threading eyes as the movement of her arms and hands lowered the instrument and her humming ceased.

"Hello Young Man of the Woods. How are you? I stand here all day and play my lyre. I have not many friends and I am trying to find one with the sounds of my music. Please, Man of the Woods, let me touch you and embrace you. Please, let me fill you with love and graceful kisses." said, the Lady with the Lyre.

"I have lived in these woods my entire life and have yet to meet you. I walked north, south, east and west and today you come to me as a wonderful surprise. I find you very beautiful and lovely to look upon. Your music plays as sweet as any I have ever heard. Please, take me into the hearth of your cabin. I will touch you tenderly and fill you with love." I proclaimed.

She held me by the hand and walked me across the threshold of her small, simple yet beautiful cabin which hosted an array of endless scents and herbs and spices. She placed me upon the softness of her bed and ran her thin fingers through my hair.

In the dash of a moment, wind hurried across the windows and through the front door. The walls rattle as decor and wind chime fell upon the wooden floor. I looked to the Lady of the Lyre and watched most terrified as she transformed from a beautiful maiden into a gruesome figure with black eyes, stringy black hair, cracked muddy skin and a withered old body.

I tried to rise from the bed and run, but I could not move.

"You cannot move, but you will in a moment. I will hunt you down, my pretty little boy, unless you find a way for me to die. A very long time ago, a very powerful demon placed a curse upon me and since then, I cannot die. There is only one way and that is to drink the shaving of the root, purple hemlock. My curse upon you, you will die if you do not kill me and you will become free when I die."

I listened to her words and thought, 'Surely, this will be an easy quest. I know an alchemist in the southern reach of the forest. I know without question, he will have the root.' Soon I loosened and freed my way from the depth of this region of the woods. I began heading south to look for a proper path to the alchemist.

Walking with speed, I arrived on the sixth day and still felt my heart pound as the sweat of my brow and back filled the shirt I wore. His name, 'Metis', hosted a small cottage near the Green river which poured into the full, beautiful valley, filled with fields and meadows. I walked tenderly through the gardens which held smooth, flat rocks and led to the front door, decorated with sigils and runes.

I tapped upon the wooden door and waited a few long moments.

"Yes." he said as he opened the door. "Oh hello, Young Man. How may I help you on this fine Autumn day?"

Upon explaining my predicament, he gave me the root of the purple hemlock as following we sat and drank a nice cup of tea. Leaving, I patted Metis upon the shoulder and thank him for the hospitality., He explained to me this root is very rare and this is the last of its kind. I trust you will use it sparingly.

Walking slower back to the Lady with the Lyre's cabin, I looked upon the root and smiled, surely my troubles should not last.

Now morning, the sky shook with shades of red, burgundy and pink. I awoke and ate and drank, then hurried along my way.

In a moments notice, I saw, standing before me, a tall red fleshed figure resembling a man. He had goat legs for legs and a black curled set of horns on his scalp. He held muscles abroad his entire body and hosted a black tail as found on a horse. I trembled in fear.

"I am a demon and I have no name, none that you can pronounce. I am the one whom placed a curse on the Lady with the Lyre. Give me the root and your life will grow long and as vast as the forest which surrounds you. You eventually will die, but sweetly and gracefully. I hold great powers and I do not like chatting with mortals. Now, hand me the root and we shall continue our own paths." said the demon.

Thinking for a brief moment, I had an idea. I slowly reached into the satchel where I held the root which, like many roots, was long and came together at a point. I withdrew the purple hemlock and in a flash, I stabbed the demon directly in the heart. He screamed a noise I have never heard before. He quaked and shook as the black bloods of him poured out in a gush. Held with terror, I gathered my things which had fallen to the floor and darted across the path in the woods to reach the home of the Lady with the Lyre.

Upon arrival, I listen to her beautiful music. She lay upon the cottons of her bed and lay nude in the form of the young beautiful woman whom I first met. She died peacefully and died with a soft smile and held the lyre in her hands. I buried her and the music continued for an everlasting time.

I smile and ducked deeply into the woods and felt warmth, deep in my heart.

Glow Rock

With the creamed yellow haze of the sun, I looked once upon the long stretch of the shadow and looked once again to the towering reach of the scattered trees. I followed the outline of the maple tree and felt the wash of the tender breeze which blossomed through every winged bud. Patterns of the stroking bark, fell as a map of the sweet gripping earth which surrounded mounds and curves of the grass beds and tosses of the snapping buds. Into the clever shout of the speeding wind, I pause at the swimming breadth of the creek and knelt to drink heavily upon the pour of the mountain gush, sweet and fragrant.

I walked further and felt a jagged sting beneath my foot. Wiping the dirt powders from the arch of my feet, looking, I saw a glowing red rock, half sunk and caked into the bed of the soil which spread past the posture of the slicing creek and still further past the bed of the softness of the sparse and flavorful woods.

I removed this relic from the crust and soil of the forest's earth. Spinning the red stone through the palms of my hands, I gasped at the glowing hues of the rock as the permeating shine danced in various dashing speeds of light when I held it to the sun. Several hours passed as the rock cast warm spears of light against me. I felt a warmth within the course of my veins. A soothing and calming emotion stretched upon me as the sun began to dip across the edge of the horizon and shadows of night bent across the fiery red treasure. As I sat mesmerized at the glowing rock, I looked around me and watched the darkness which turned to light, held the silhouettes of persons motioning toward me in a reaching grasp. Whether I knew them, I did not know, but the congregation of the sauntering ghosts spread through the edges of woods which quietly surrounded me. I watched the phantoms and the beam colored persons as the nearby trees washed and soothed against the trembling cauldron of burgundy and soft pinks and the dash of heavy marbling wine shades.

I had been awake for days and I felt no need for sleep. There reached no occasion for eating, plenty of food surrounded me, as my desires for necessities seemed to drift and course it's way upon the melding colors and blooming shadows. I, The Boy of the Woods, felt soft and calm as the days passed. As a tremble of the pouring rain, fell upon me and turned swiftly to a sizzle where the steam and fog, rose from my pale skin, I breathed the scents of the most distant and remote fullness of the far fields and the nearby gathering of the patch of mint and the sweet tug of peach roses and burst of the grape hyacinth.

More days passed and I heard the persons sing, chant and moan as the shuffling leaves caress the flesh of me as the excitement of my mind stimulated across everything that lived in this section of the sweetest woods. The winds spoke of lucidity as each gust trembled across the angles and curves of my soft body. The female motions spoke of a yearning to suckle and to reach upon the children whom slept in the most gentle poise. Each of the tangled roots and weeds beneath the earth, longed to coddle me in beds of grasses and full stretches of the soil in the field and meadow.

I felt something in my throat, something satisfying which went to the midst of my hollow belly. I felt drink, water, for the first time in several days. Swiftly, I awoke and saw my old friend Metis standing before me. He wore a burlap shirt and a loose pair of khaki pants. Around his neck rested a symbol of the goddess of the woods, one which I have witnessed many times before. In his hand, he held a spoon and upon my knees sat a bowl of oatmeal. He held a bladder of cool water which slid down my throat and edged as sharp tools, reopening my passageway where I desired most fervently.

I had been broken from the spell which I had recently thought was a blessing, yet turned to reach me in the near hour of my death. Metis, the apothecary and I, held a blossoming friendship which remained far and near. We loved each other with the pulses within.

"I almost lost you, The Young Boy of the Woods. I dreamed of your curse, spell rather and set out to save you before it swelled across you final grip. Are you feeling better?" softly spoke Metis, the apothecary.

Weakly, I spoke, "Where rests the rock?"

"I had to take it and put in a realm where it can no longer be found." said Metis.

I looked around and the rock went as Metis had said. There was a surprising sigh of relief which came from the depth of my lungs. Shaking with terror from the encounter which had surpassed, I ate more and drank more then stood, only to fall upon the ground in exhaustion.

"You need to rest. I will be here by your side as the several days pass. Here, take a blanket and relish in the warmth of this drink." exclaimed the apothecary, Metis.

I took a deep drink which tasted like a Summer peach and lulled my breath to a calming chant as I slid into the blossoms of sleep.

I awoke to the sound of the lovebird and the morning lark. The moist earth bathed me in gentleness and pauses of freshness upon my clothes. Sunshine dances through the leaves of the trembling forest and softened upon my face and skin. My belly held no room and I felt as if I drank several bladders the coldest water. Slowly, I stood and remained upon my legs. The creek pored slow and cast my reflection which stood in perfect resemblance.

Looking around me, I saw the wavering, flicker of the ferns and the well spread bundle of the moss which hooked to the reaching trees and the open portions of the covered rocks. I held the balance of all which surrounded me and calmly, I began to sing songs of far away lands and the troubled stories of the troubled seas. Then, looking behind me, Metis patted me with his palm and smiled at me.

"I must tell you, this rock must be destroyed. Take it to the Majestic Oak and plant it deep in its roots. Only the Oak can smother the magic which the rock holds. This relic of a rock comes from the heart of a Witch and belongs to rest somewhere safe. The rock belongs to you, I have placed it at the bottom of your backpack and you must do this before nightfall. Please, my friend, hurry." said Metis

"I will. I will find you soon, perhaps at your cottage in the Woods." replied The Young Boy of the Woods.

I grabbed my backpack, a bladder full of water and my favorite hiking stick and made haste for the deep meadows beyond the woods where the Magic Oak Tree rested. The heavy sky grew the darkest shade of charcoal as the winds pounded with a flurry of drops. I pressed heavy as I could sense the encounter I approached with the Witch.

Far to the distance rests the Oak. I could hear her chant, "Hurry Young Boy, she's right behind you. Hurry, place the rock in the depth of my soil." exclaimed the Magic Oak.

I was almost at length to where the soil remained soft. With a dive, I landed upon the soil and plunged it well into the depth of the earth. I looked back and the Witch, who was young and beautiful, swiftly turned into ashes and the earth moaned in a rumble as her body and garments faded upon the wind.

"Leave the glow rock where it rests. It will be safe with me." spoke the gentle tree.

I left and walked for several days, eating and smiling along the way as I slowly turned a corner which presented me to the home of Metis. I could hear the crickets sing and the locust' burrow through the near bush and the near tree. There my friend sat on the edge of his wooden porch. He simply looked to me and said, "Welcome back."

Nymph of the Lake

The lake sulked and breathed fog and mist which blended into the thin cobalts and foamed whites which held and slithered across the edge, until today which sauntered upon the nakedness of her slender body and once she left I witnessed her lovingly. Travelling my way through the treetops, then later, upon the softest mosses which threaded along the ground, I watched her as she sustained the heavy blue and roped, tangled whites. As night lingered forth, she went into the closest meadow and danced in the quivering moonlight. She danced further and faded into the thick wheats and trembling barley. By the peak of midnight, I realized she held no shadow and gently, she passed beyond the edges of the glen.

As the wind approached with whistling blooming clouds which fell close to the majesty of the sweet earth, the heavy breeze cast moans and tender laughter upon the strain of my keen hearing and the touch of her voice suckled me forth across the reaching fields. At a swift pace, I sliced through the grains and coated myself in loosened pollens and seeds which pressed upon the leather of my boots and calves. I looked upon the starlit sky and the moonlit trembling dances where the wheat shuffled before me. I watched as the trees lightly scattered across the trembling grasses of the glen bowed and ushered me forth.

Upon walking across the shaking weeds and ferns beneath my feet, I felt the warm breath of the sky and the coming rains which will tickle the fertile earth. As I stood in stillness, I heard her sultry, young voice dance across the fields. I could not hear the words which where edging from her throat and mouth, but it came from the western creek. I scurried in a dash.

Walking through the rains as the earth suckled it's way into the cakes of the rainy soil and crust, I rushed as quickly as the trail allowed me to scurry. The aromas and loosening powders of her, cast upon the air and fell upon me in a tender flash of lusty, raw flesh. Into the quivering slice of the coveting creek which coddles upon the slouch of the carved, slippery, rocky beds, I ever so faintly heard the sweetest voice which came further from the west and with lusty moans positioned me in a feverish freeze.

Her scent which sauntered as a distinction in the breath of the earth, motioned me to continue through the approaching forest, which lured me into a trembling shake of each faculty of my eager body, I followed the fall of the flower petals which she givingly left sparse upon the woodland path.

Hurrying forth, I ran and looked all around me as the trees stayed still and the wind blew fast across the canopy of the pines and I looked upon the bushes and vines as they threaded their roots deeply into the earth. The closer I came to finding her, the stronger her perfect voice and perfect breath swabbed across me and the sooner I pictured her in my mind, the more I swallowed the burden of this temptation. Suddenly, I realized, I stood in the center of the woods and the air grew quiet and everything around me and in attention, all groomed the wind and all made no sound.

Her fragrance lofted across the stillness of the sweeping forest breath and tenderly, I looked across this wooded cove and saw her standing in lust and tremoring beauty which shook through me as the moonlit glazes of the leaves and pine cones lay gathered around her. Her hair and fingers exotically held the color white. From her neck to her ankles in all different shades of the color blue, her breasts motioned the palest and thickened in a surrounding as the rest of the curves deepened in darker hues. Her feet coated in the color of a dark chestnut and her face tempted in the shades of apricot. I could not tell her length in years, but I witnessed no beauty such as hers in all my years of living. As she stood before me, I watched her in a heavy freeze and noticed the glint of her smile.

"I am the Nymph of the Lake'," she said in her well pitched soothing voice.

"I am The Young Boy of the Woods," I replied in all humble sincerity.

As she approached me I stood motionless and burned in desire which brought me to a quivering halt directly before she touched me upon the lips and leaned across and kissed me upon the redness of my cheeks. I felt the blood of myself begin to rush through me and my body moved in fluency and proper direction. In a gushing, sweet quiver, I said,

"I find you to be remarkably beautiful. Standing before me, I quake to your very touch. More than any other, I desire you and love you. Each night for the past cycle of the moon, I watch you at your lake. But tonight was different. Tonight you have no shadow. How did it disappear?" I spoke slowly and delicately.

"My shadow was taken with a curse which was tossed upon me. An evil creature of the forest stole my shadow and I can bear no children until I have my shadow back. The creature, half goat and half man resides in these woods. If you truly find me beautiful and you would like me to love you, assuredly, I will be yours," she spoke so eloquently. "I will be on the island in the middle of the lake."

"I do love you and I will find your shadow. Please, wait for me and I will give you a child." I replied softly and will confidence.

She, before leaving, gave me a kiss on the redness of my cheek. As I stood overwhelmed in tender, yet acute sensations, I looked upon the rising sun. I began my hunt.

Sitting upon a fallen log, I felt my mind brew as I searched for a plan, or direction to start. I knew there lived a wiseman near here. He aged very slowly and lived in a reclusive lifestyle. He lived alone and was only a few miles from her; I did not know the way perfectly, but with my knowledge of the woods, I felt a decent chance of finding him. He went by the name, "The Wiseman." His brethren respected him quite thoroughly as did his elders, those whom have passed and still call upon him.

Having no other place to turn, I will find him and call upon his wisdom and thoughts.

As I came upon his campsite, entertaining only a small tent and a campfire pit which rested near a small brook, filled with trout and freshwater. Again, it smothered the sky in darkness as it spread in nightfall. He sat next to the small crackling fire and hummed a tune which threaded through his mind in complacency and cooperation. He wore a soft, silk shirt and a pair of loose burlap pants. He wore a medallion around his neck which held a design I have never seen before. The smoke from the fire spindled through the air and weaved through the trees. Adjacent to the high reaching tree, molded of red maple, his staff rested and gave off a very sweet odor and a clever green aura.

"The Wiseman," I said in a very calm direction. "I come to you needing knowledge and advise. Is there anything I could do to arouse your thoughts? I have a carafe of wine if it would please you?"

"Please sit down and please fill my cup with a bit of wine. I am always eager for an interesting visitor and to please you with honestly, it has been a very long time. So please, sit down before me and we can converse." The Wiseman, replied softly.

We sat and talked for many hours about many different things. We spoke of the woods, the lake, the restless behavior of the forest, and the beauty of, 'The Nymph of the Lake." He assured me 'The Evil Creature of the Woods' lived in the forest to the north, above the roaming fields of wheat and barley. He gave me his sacred staff and taught me a magical line as the flushing power surged through me and I felt a tremor of delight. This magical staff would steal back the shadow of the Nymph and abolish the Evil Creature to the darkness of the Underworld which will bind him for all eternity. The Wiseman stood and patted me on the shoulder and went into his tent for sleep. I thanked him and said goodbye.

It was now midday, the next morning and I reached the fields of thick roaming wheat. From here, I headed north and caught sight of the Northern Forest. I found a trail which burrowed through the barley fields and headed for the woods. Now it was late afternoon and the woods which shrouded me stood thick and held the light to the sky as each occasional flickering leaf answered as just enough for me to see my way. I could smell, almost taste, the minerals of the sweetly shrouded earth. As I walked through the depth of the woods, the staff began to glow the brightest of colors in the shades and hue of the color green.

I heard a horrible sound of laughter and wrath as the Evil Creature of the Woods, stood before me. He picked up a thin, razor sharp sword and swung it upon me with all his might and speed. As I ducked, I spilled out the magical chant and pointed the staff directly at the Evil Creature. In an instant, he swelled and screamed in agony. A massive light struck the Evil Creature and quickly he fell upon the earth of the forest bed and turned pale only to wither upon the tender earth.

We lay next to each other as the sun cast her soft shadow across the island and filled me

Me with tension and flooding postures. Sweet dampness of her abdomen and curving breasts lay heavy upon the perch of my heavy waist to my thrashing groin. We stay here until a full cycle of the moon cast the tender sun upon us.

Western Reach

Once I walked in the forest of oak trees far in the depth of the western reach which caressed in the valley far beyond the Great Mountains of the iced peaks and rock laden paths. I opened my lungs and the quiver of my chilled spine as the gathering mounds of leaves spooled upon the gentle floor of these lazy woods, sweetly alive as every leaf covered me in the moan of a shroud, these tender dusts of Autumn. The sky spread as an open vein of the blood which tempered a dying warmth upon me and filled the dome of the heavens, sweet and gloating in October purity. I positioned myself on the high rock which cast my sight along the vast tangle of the oak and the thin wash of jade green grasses and burrowing thickets. Walking through the woods with eager interest and eager desire, I looked for my lost, loved friend who once ruled as the crowned King of Autumn, now, he lost his path in the deep of the oak and through the western reach of the Kingdom. We rested and bonded together as the blood of two brothers would rest. He, King of Autumn and I, the young Boy of the Woods was his brother. He vanished and I must find him.

Being many years my elder, I felt the loving care and touch of his laid path of guidance which taught, blossomed and educated me both in the rules of the wilderness and the path of hosting myself to the strength of brotherhood and fellowship. I recall every leaf and map of the bark which spoke upon the trembling sweet aroma, speaking and filling myself with direction and soft words as the sweet flavors called upon me. When the rain would pound upon the earth, I heard the moans of ghosts and phantoms which trembled in the falling tears of the sky and left the stain of the mourning of the deceased, soft and tender with the sobbing fields and the soaking overflow of the creeks and rivers, I heard each pant and groan through the gestures of the wind. Tenderly, he taught me how to sing the sweetest songs and how to write beautiful love poems which caressed the hearts of the nymphs of the woods which would in turn open the floodgates and desires and passions would thicken and tremble between us. He lovingly showed me the animals which tenderly traveled the path of the feral beast and the calming pauses of the birds and rabbits and all which scurried for food and drink. He, my elder, showed me the love between brothers and the guidance of my fellow man. I received word from a nymph from these woods and I dashed in a hurry and motioned my way through his land and swiftly, I am on the hunt for his safety and establishment.

My brother's name hasn't been used in many years, decades as he now ruled this section of the western reach. His name was, 'Doran Child of the Woods.' Now, he simply went by, 'King of the Western Reach'. He loved all which lived in the coddling safety of the oaks and the perfection of every leaf which fell and gathered upon the ferns, mosses and roots and weeds, high and alive in the toss of the winds. When Autumn arrived in early September and departed at the later reach of November, he held plays, poetry forums and festivals which positioned him as beloved and respected most high above all. Now, the last day of August, he faded, disappeared, or simply fell to the richness of the earth and I sensed trembling fear among his people and subjects.

With my green glowing staff, snug and fitted in the grip of my coarse leathery hands, I walked from the southernmost ridges where rocky ledges scattered stones and pebbles across the sudden dusty cliffs. Opening my mouth to the clean and vibrant sleek air which filled my lungs with a calmness and soft presence, I traveled my way to the center of the wood of the oak trees. Along the way, I passed many creatures, such as: squirrels, rabbits, foxes, raccoons, mice, chipmunks, deer, elk and bears. I looked to the treetops and watched: blackbirds, crows, ravens, turkey vultures, blue birds, a charm of goldfinches, rens, cardinals and doves. As I stopped along the path and spoke to each creature looking for clues and hints as to where my brother, the King, remained at the current time, the answer always remained bleak and distant from acute direction. The sound of night in the Oak Woods, trembled upon me with the chants of the crickets and grasshoppers, the locust and the deep evening 'caw' of the crow.

I stopped by a large oak which reach high and broad as the branches moaned with the steady passage of the wind. Leaning upon the trunk, I felt my head brew into a swirl from the scampering breath fallen from the sky dome and the quick trample of my burning feet. Slowly, I fell further and further into the land of dreams. Almost, I swept across the distant lands of trees, fields, creeks and meadows, I heard a soft voice which threaded and trembled upon me and I woke in a fast scurry.

I looked around myself and called out, "Hello, who's there? I am The Young Boy of the Woods. Please, tell me who you are?"

"I am the Nymph of the Forest of the Western Reach." said the tree which caressed me with her leaves. "Do you seek your brother, The King?'

"Indeed, I do. Do you know where I can find him? Is he alive?" I proclaimed with a touch of calm desperation.

She replied, "Yes he lives and yes, I know where you can find him. Just as me, he has been turned into a great oak tree. He stays trapped in the furthest edge of the western stance of the Western Reach. He sleeps as the last tree of the woods before the meadows reach and touch the sea."

"May I sleep a bit here with you, Nymph of the Western Reach," I asked soothingly.

"Of course. Before you alter your brother back to his former person, you will need a relic which will ensure the change. In the cave of madness, which holds horrible creatures of the dark, there is a staff, much like yours, but it glows the color yellow," she explained calmly.

"Where is this cave?" I asked.

"Five miles precisely north of here. I do not know what creatures are in there, be careful," she said with renewed calmness.

I slept a bit and dreamed dreams of hope. I saw my brothers face, alive with a smile as the winds rustled the branches and leaves fell and I awoke to the scents of morning.

With speed, I traveled to the north, making a straight line looking for the cave of madness which held the secret to saving my brother and the Nymph of the Western Reach. As I came upon the cave, I detected a scent which would turn the stomach of a witch, or perhaps a demon. The cave, in my sight, cast such a pungent aroma, I bent forward and vomited upon the grasses before me. I walked slowly and peered inside. A large red colored bull which was loosely chained to the wall of the cave stood with wrath and a touch of madness, much as the cave has been named. I peered into the layout and saw a distant yellow glow which lurked from the back of the cave.

Under duress, I dug into my backpack and removed a piece of dried meat. Tossing the flesh across the floor, I watched as the bull scampered for it and began his feast. I darted in a flash and ran to the yellow staff which leaned against the far wall. I snatched the staff with my right hand and quickly turned to the exit of the cave. I could feel my stomach churn as I went to scurry out the exit.

The bull slowly, with drool upon the mouth, turned and faced me with fury. I fastened the green staff in my opposite hand and conjured the magical word and sent a charge of energy to snap at the mad bull. The charge crashed against the flesh of the bull and stunned him with just enough time in which I could escape. I heard the roaring bull for many miles as I fled to the most western reach where my brother was being held captive.

My brother, the nymph and I walked splendidly across the great oak forest. We stopped and aroused the court and the people of the woods to have a banquet and festival of sweet sounding music.

The evil creature who caused this trouble, we did not find. Perhaps this will become aware to us at another time.

The Eldar and the Creature
of the Southern Woods

Once, I sat before him. He replied to every one of my questions with perfection and serenity, perhaps simple kindness. He, 'The Elder of the Great Woods', reigned the forest with wisdom and brilliant insight as well as a sincere love of every creature, person, tree, weed and rock with loving duplicity from one to another. He called upon me with concern for my health and well being, when at the time, I sat and remained confused and tense. This audience stood honest and truthful while the danger of the future burdened before me in rising tremor and fear.

He sat calmly before the crackling embers of his campfire. He heated water and mixed it with shredded tea leaves. Sipping the tea with slow, irresistible enjoyment, I looked upon him and noticed his burlap coat, well stitched leather pants, long hair pulled in many braids and a medallion when looked at could make one dizzy with multiple interpretations. His skin color gleamed pale and at first drew upon an insight of weakness and frailty. With further sensing, he sat and stared far into the void with a strength which reach all in fortitude and perfection. At last, The Elder of the Great Woods, turned to look upon me and spoke, "I fear for you, my friend, 'The Young Boy of the Woods'. You have great strength in your heart, yet a darkness of great power shrouds you. When I look into your eyes, I sense joy and a young man of friendship and loving kindness. When I look at your burning aura, I sense the power of darkness hunts you for his delicious joy.

"Far to the south, across the crystal river, deep in the southern forest lives a creature of power and evil. This creature stands tall, broad and strong. He wears a gnarled furry coat and holds great devil horns upon his skull. His torso and legs are that of a mighty steed. His arms are great and fierce as he stands upon two rear legs which carry him with swiftness. In the left hand, he carries a long whip which holds razors upon the ends. In his right hand, he carries a great sword which stretches the length of a large grown man. Being able to see miles into the distance with keen clarity whether in the daytime or nighttime, might prove to be your enemy.

"Now you may wonder, 'Why does this creature want to hunt you?' He is the one who placed your brother, The King of the Western Reach, under his curse and turned him into a mighty oak tree, as well as the 'Nymph of the Western Reach'. Ages ago, as children, the Creature and your brother fought over the same young nymph. Your brother, The King, exiled him from the Western Reach. Over the years, 'The Creature of the Southern Forest', broke the spell of your brother with magic he stole from me. That will rest as a tale for another time." said the calm words of the Elder of the Great Woods.

I sat for a terribly long time and tried to relax myself as words and comments spun through my mind. At last, I drew a deep breath and looked at the Elder and said, "What shall I do. It seems this 'Evil Creature of the Southern Forest' will tear me to shreds in an instant? I have my green and yellow hiking staves. Will they provide me with any type of edge, or advantage?" I said without being able to hide from my fears.

"No said the Elder. He will prove superior above even those strong gifts. I will give you a potion which will turn you invisible for an interval of Dusk to dawn when the bloods of pink and red flood the morning sky. This beast grows more powerful by the day. You must strike him in the heart with his mighty sword."

"I will do my best to conquer this creature. I feel the need to ask you a question. Why are these trials I have been undergoing seemingly relentless and cruelly stationed at myself?" I asked with truth and sincerity.

The Elder, replied, "Only your ancestors can reveal an answer such as that. Here, take your potion and please don't forget food and drink. By the hour of dawn, you must be on your path. As I have my fire and my medallion, I will do all I can to keep you safe."

The sky spread beautifully to the east as the gray night clouds faded in perfect dissolution. I took a lesser known path from the campfire meeting which still rang clearly in my seemingly tender and terrified mind. I passed a thin patch of onion root which tangled upon my nose and choked slightly upon my edgy throat. Threading through that, I arrived upon a lavender bush which soaked my senses in a calm quiver. Going passed a curving bend in the road, the sweet flare of a mint patch swiftly exhilarated my fears and drew me to a series of refined memories in which the aroma of mint brought past fun and joy.

I traveled with speed, partly from an eagerness to meet this treachery and to end this creature's life and partly to end mine if the ancestors will have it this way. By the time I entered the Southern woods and crossed the Crystal River, I felt a musty foul smelling, wavering air descend upon me. The sun had climbed it's way across the dome of heaven and slowly unburdoned into the nest of the western mesh which returned the favor of the morning caress. The pungent stench of the surrounding woods climbed across me and lathered me with an intense fear. The sky stood seconds near dark as I removed the potion which caused invisibility. This potion surprisingly had no odor and upon drinking, had no taste other than the flavor of a fresh spring creek.

As I passed my way through the woods here to the south, I caught notice of a great maple tree which held an engraving upon the thickness of the bark. I gasp for breath as I realized this engraving was the same as the Elder's medallion. A sense of renewed faith swept across me. The scent in these woods grew worse as pulses within my blood fastened me to a slight fastening of hope. I slowly continued on as the scent gripped me in sickness and I heaved and pressed the air for something a bit more clean. I looked across an empty grotto of the thick section of the woods and I noticed another engraving of the same source. The Elder's claim to help must have reigned true.

I scanned my sight east and west. Surely two more engravings fastened upon the two maple trees. Although, I did not know what these signs meant, they reassured me I am not entirely alone.

Looking upon myself, I came to the awareness, I stood on this cursed forest and indeed, I stood invisible to the wealth of woods which surrounded me. I stopped and curiously wondered, 'Can I be felt?' I placed my hands upon the flesh of my body and paused to realize, I certainly can. I felt the speed in which my blood began pumping and felt a dryness in my still fearful self.

The creature stood from behind a large rock which centered in the grotto. He appeared exactly as the Eldar had described with the only difference remaining edged across me as the amount of terror this beast spread around him. Although

I stood still and terrified, I had to think of something. He said at last, "I can smell you. Where do you hide? I will let you live if you remove this spell. I cannot move from this grotto. Who are you that you can use such ancient magic.

I caught myself breathing heavier and quickly tried to calm myself so I could remain silent. I quickly Removed my hunting knife from my pocket and entertained the idea that I will sever the sword from his hand. "'I must be quick,'" I thought. Just then, an owl 'cooed' through the woods slightly beyond. I dashed and dove upon the arm which wielded the mighty sword. Just before I carved the knife upon his wrist, he grabbed me by the collar bone and tossed me directly in front of him. He swung the sword and missed me by a slight inch. I heard from behind me a mighty growl. I sliced through in another chance and managed to carve about half of his wrist. The scream became worse as the sword fell to the earth and I witnessed a tangle of dust climb upon the air.

Much as the Eldar had told me at the campfire, the Creature of the Southern Woods lay dead before me. I stood still and silent while I watched the body of the Creature of the Southern Woods crumble and fasten to dust. The horrific scent began to fade and the weapons sank deeply into the earth. I look for the engravings on the tree and took notice they had vanished leaving no trace or blemish upon the wood.

Sitting with the Eldar of the Woods, I ate beautifully tasting food and drank finely aged wine. We rejoiced in the defeat of the creature and eagerly awaited the accompaniment of the Nymph of the Western Woods and my brother, The King of the Western Reach. Well into the next evening, we laughed and told tales of our exploits.

The pursuit of my need to confer with my ancestors awaited me. I will pursue this further.

Greatest of Ancestors

Once, in the blaze of Summer heat, the sweat of the salted rivers caressed the burn of my temples and neck, chest and back. Wading ankle deep through the bounty of the ferns which swarm across the rock filled forest, spread boulders which slump as moss covered landmarks which lulled me to laziness and tender exhaustion. I swiftly steamed my way across the dark, heavy slabs as each crunched beneath my leather boots. Each bead of sweat suckled across the chill of my back and tangled winds swept my soft face and motioned my hair with every move of laughter. Deep roots of the various, scattered trees plunged into speared treasures of the earth and spoke to me of our blood and marrow. Now, on my way to the distant meadow which humbly rests north of the Northern Reach, the trim of the forest stretched thinner and more giving of the fertile lusty soil which held myself in a most pleasant way.

I have been named, "The Young Boy of the Woods." My parents I remember only slightly and at a young age. I recall being given to the farmer as far to the east which still rests and now holds the deceased in the loose soil on the land he served. I am sure he had a name, but I remember him as, "The Farmer of the East". I know not why my parents abandoned me. I serve the woods, meadows, the hills and the majesty of the mountain. The sound of the barn owl and the 'caw' of the murder of crows, swift passage of the deer and the tenderness of the gazelle all breath across me and eventually, I speak with them in all soothing floods of friendship. I gather every nut, the walnut, acorn and the luxury of the pecans and place them in my pouch.

The day aroused me when the winds tore through the fields and shook me of my farthest dream into the realm of my ancestors. I awoke in the hustle of morning and all was dark. The sky grew as a canvas and tossed every shade of darkness across me. I stood and stirred with fear as the grass steered as a parallel and caught the slapping raindrops which trembled in a robbery of moisture. After looking for the slight rim of the new moon, I saw black. Knowing the near hickory tree, I scampered and found the base as I brought my knees to my chest and placed my arms around my knees. The thought of magic slipped into my mind. For a great length of time I reached into the furthest depths of my knowledge of the villages, towns, buildings, and constructs which rested upon the spread of this most tender meadow. I listened to the gnashing sounds of the storm, the spearing rush of the ferocious stream which gushed a short mile behind me. The nearby village rested silent as the wind swept through huts, buildings and barns leaving a soft resounding hollow of silence where the farmers, tavern folk and smithies once would hustle through the day. I listened through the smash of the sky as the nearest town cracked, smashed and tumbled upon the thick of the spreading mud sulked each construct into the deep of the earth.

As I look to the eye of the madness of the storm, lathering in mud, I sensed a center of calmness which hosted the wild pressing storm. Feeling the press of this burrowing majestic crux where I haunched and sensed the cause of the madness,

I came to the conclusion that there stooped a high reaching tower which bloomed the storm which attacked every edge of the meadow with the threat of devastation lulling closer upon the life which tenderly neared the brink of vanishment.

From a far reaching distance came a voice which swept and overtook the heavy sounds of the surrounding tempest. With an initial slam of a piercing voice, I heard a full, brash tempo and scattered pitch which brushed across me and left shivering in trembling fear. I felt the scars of the earth beg me for softness and eagerly looking for healing tenderness.

Finally, I gathered the sounds and listened to the menace of this tremor and lashing wickedness. "Your powers reach much deeper than I had initially thought. I am the 'Great Wizard of the East'. I must say, you have wandered far from your realm where you roam the depths of the earth. I understand you listen, speak to the moans and voices of the marrow of your ancestors. As a champion to the woodlands where you belong, you reach yourself as fearless and dash from demon, monster, and witch.

"I must say, you will be a prize treasure in the cavern of my keep. Greater treasures than you have found their path in the dungeon where I will carve you into the statue which will grip each edge of your flesh and bone. Silent, motionless accompaniment will freeze by you as your sweet, tender soul which will shatter with every moment as you look upon your ancestors whom fill in each crack and mortar as an empty speech will vibrate across you. With assurance, these ancestors are not just any, or mundane persons at best. They are your parents, The Young Boy of the Woods. I will lather in the horror of the macabre eternity you will spend with them. I am the Great Wizard of the East. Spend some time, perhaps more than you should. In the end, I know you shall arrive," said the Great Wizard of the East.

I felt my anger brew and fester through the dark burgundy of my thickening blood. I couldn't simply walk to the keep and present myself as that would prove a definite end.

The wild storm continued as I heard the cries of the fallen bellow out across each direction of every edge of this once tender and beautiful land. All animals fled and deepened into the forest and did so with speed and vigor. The streams and rivers swelled full as they suckled every grass blade and soaked each fern patch and spread of moss. Fields of full wheat tamped their stretch into the mud of the earth with sacred moaning and burrow of every sunken seed. The oak trees snapped and shouted with a crackling scream. I could see the ages of the wood as the rings mourned upon the near earth and slicked grass. With sweet vibrations of the wind and the sky, I heard the twisting floods pour from the heavens. An idea came to my mind like a flash of lightning which jousted from the sky.

On my way to the vast, large town, I went to meet a wizard who made her dwelling in this town called, 'Sillsberg'. Her name, 'Sweet Velvet' swept across this region and held tenderness and power with each whom know her and have heard of her. She claimed a posture of the definitive majestic prowess which I very much needed to defeat the Great Wizard of the East.

On the path to the town which rested upon the summit of the sweet rolling hills, filled with spruce and rows of peach roses, I thought so deeply of my parents whom I truly did not really know. I understood they were treasures of the Great Wizard, being that they held a charm of the majesty of the charisma of the forest and all it claimed. I also knew he wanted me as his next trophy, a statue in the deep of his wealth and museum.

In a few long and arduous days, I reached the town which stood and held ravished as I keenly expected. Walking at a quickened pace, I searched for the place of Sweet Velvet. At first, I couldn't detect the senses I obtain from a powerful wizard, nor the building structure which one of the sort would choose for a proper fitting. With a sudden finding, I came upon the grotto of the town which held a beautiful fountain centered upon the highest reach of the tender rolling hills. The house stood and made it's structure of stone and wood as the peaks held an array of slender metal gables. Small metal monsters perched upon the sides of the gate which led into the large door at the front of the house. As I walked near the door, I smelled a sweet fragrance which swooned my head and fastened my knuckles to the posture of this keep.

There I stood with no answer after the tap of my knock. As panic began to rush through me, I wiped glazes of sweat from my forehead and the contours of my face. As I proceeded to knock at a more rapid rate, I looked upon the ground in defeat. There sat a small wooden box with the name, The Young Boy of the Woods, written upon it. Knelt, the box contained a necklace which held the stones: a ruby, sapphire, opal, onyx and emerald. I did the obvious and placed the necklace around my neck. In an instant, I faded, disappeared. I could feel myself and what things I encountered, but I was transparent, invisible to the world around me. I wished to thank Sweet Velvet, but I am sure she had her business helping the town which was on the brink of destruction.

I could feel the thrusting pangs of madness which arrived from the keep so far into the cascading rains of the meadow, alive with an eagerness to crush and mold me into a soul trap, a receptacle of fastened spirits and flesh. My leather wrapped boots sulked and sank into the mud and soaked grass as the raindrops stung my face as needles slung from the apex of the sky. Wincing in pain, yet further, I trudged across the fields of mud approaching the keep in the scourge of my madness and wrath. The smell of the boned rib of the earth trembled across me and flurried through me into my lungs and tastes upon my mouth and tongue. I smelled age as the countless bones splintered against the smashing lightning, blue and cobalt blue; the weakening of the shedding flesh, the drip of the sweet marrow tossed me into an ancestral absence. I pressed forward as the black sky swabbed and coated me in blankets of descension.

Finally, I entered the eye of the storm. Before me, struck deeply in the ground and reaching as high as the softened clouds, stood the keep of the Great Wizard of the East. The keep stood in the reach of a square holding towers in the palms of each corner and hosted a flag meshed the colors black and purple. As I faced the front of the giant structure, there stood rounded double doors which met the height, twenty feet high and fifteen feet wide. I stood in stillness and watched; I looked across the structure only to witness the storm faded and the skies of the great meadow cleared. I've climbed the greatest trees and crossed the most mighty boulders, now I will top the keep and face the terror of my fate, success or destruction.

I grabbed each nook, edge, and stone as I reached the peak of the keep which held rocks cornered with the most slippery of rocks and the sleek coat of the moss and tremble from the winds as the walk became a balancing act.

"Up to tricks I see. Let us strike a deal, I will let you leave with your life if you hand over the token which carved you into foggy dissipation, transparency, invisibility. You hold more power than I thought at first when I watched you on your excursions and travels, demons and witches. Your instincts and ancestors brought you here, now it will reign as time for us to cooperate. I shall leave a loud painful buzz upon your ears which will ring in your head until I have that necklace," exclaimed the Great Wizard of the East.

I spoke out loud, "You are a fool. I hold much more magic than this small supple necklace. I will be the first to admit you hold vast powers, but also the first to admit you are but a cowardly fool."

I searched the rooftop and found a door laying flat upon the rock floor. Traveling downward, I searched for the dungeon the basement. The stinging noise pierced through my head and left me with a shattering headache. I felt that at any moment, I would collapse and turn into a collective piece in his dungeon museum.

Upon entering the dungeon, I witnessed statues abroad which absorbed my eyesight and then still, my head pounded harder.

"I must admit, your trick is clever and I must admit, I cannot see you. You have found your way to my treasures and this will not stand. Give me the necklace or I will turn you into a block of stone," proclaimed the Great Wizard.

In a moment, my will for subtlety had come to an end. I removed the hunting knife from my pocket and slung forward into an attack. I stabbed the knife deeply into the neck of the Great Wizard. Blood spilled as an open casket upon the depth of the floor. Hot blood covered me as I trembled in victory.

So I heard the voices unison, "We did not abandon you my son. Indeed we love you. We were trapped as a treasure for the Great Wizard. We used the last of our powers to place you in the woodlands far away. I, your father, my name is Virgil and me, your mother, my name is Octavia. The ancestors are calling us to join them. When you speak to the ancients, we will be there. Remember my son, keep to the woods.

Death of the Fair Lady
of the Woods

Once, on a perfectly risen Autumn day, I breathed every sweet mineral and spice of the earth and tenderly, I spoke to the blackbirds and the charm of finches. Moisture of the soft willing soil spoke of the near and swift river which tunneled through the depth of the eager forest. Upon listening to the slapping waters and the discrete driftwood which sliced through every rapid and curve, I heard the stone wood speak of antiquity and blossoming winds, edging the current to the softening sides, spread upon the grasses and ferns.

As I approached the river, coated with the colors of blue and blue cobalt, the goldfinches peppered the sweet flurry of October winds which held a backdrop of amber skies and wedges of peach roses which made the heavens a distinct declaration of this somber evening. With a racing flock of blackbirds came the rise and conquer of the drench of nightfall; the slippery, cool haste of the falling leaves pampered the edges and the rest of the year of the forest floor. I sat along the moss covered boulders which sank deeply in the woodland soil. The small limber branches held up among the current of the sweet source where breathing winds needled me as I walked through the tremoring display of the sweetest passage of wilts, the snare of the tree branches and adjudication of this Autumn sky whipped me in heavy breath of the forest and forest earth.

Cool sweat trickled down my back and softened my heated flesh as I stepped along the small, red and ivory colored bridge. Looking upon the underdraft of the clear water, I watched as the trout quivered in measure of the fast, darting stream, swift and transparent spoke to me of the pebbles which have been asleep here for thousands.

After finding the mountain path which tore upon the earth and led to the peak of the stretch of the Southern Mountain. I filled my mouth with the crystal water and tightened my leather boots. I grabbed the yellow staff and tied my hair back as the wind swept upon me and propelled the cool sweat, resting upon my back. Moments past, I spoke to the emerald shades of moss. With every patch upon every tree, the moss spoke of a phantom which rests and lurks upon the mountain crests and peaks. They spoke of the tender, sweet wind which swoons upon me and the madness of nightfall which hosts the phantom and holds as a foundry, all the venom of the powers of black night. I thought my way to the emerald moss, 'Does this phantom haunt me and if so why does this phantom haunt me, pursue me?'

Standing still, I closed my eyes and pictured the swirling wind, the snap of the branch and toss of the crippled leaf. I watched a marvel of foggy mist which blends well upon the rocky plateau and whispers thrashing attacks which spread from this transparent haze, open upon the dancing breath of this stirring, cruel figment. I smiled weakly and placed a crumpling leaf upon a of moss and gently turned my way.

Upon the path, I heard the squirrels tunnel along the edges of the trees, the red fox in all it's handsome charm swerved along the bushes and plants and the dash of the gazelle which along the breath of me as the winds spoke of softness and tenderness. At the first reach of the tangling path, born of thicket and thorns, I watched the fade of the sky and stepped nearer to the cherry tree and the fall of the petals which filled me with fear. A light stabbing rain flooded the dirt wedge at the bottom of the neat wedge of the leather upon my feet.

Steep, the gravel and dusty rock scattered path climbed in an upward slant; I too walked in a angeled hike with a sting in my ribs and a hot burn in my legs. Drifting fog suckled each shard of life as each wavering press wept upon me and spoke to me of the venom which currently sinks deep into the earth. With every crimp of every leaf and fading inch of woodland life, The phantom floated and grooved into the fade of the conquer where the wallowing howl of each depressed of death fell to the basin of the floor high upon the rocky path.

Amidst the wrath which dried and gathered the mountain and all the spreading forest, I paused and looked about. Within moments, I found myself deep in the patterns and heavy gambits of thought. I thought of the phantom and all it's mystic as the trembling motions flooded the motions of weaving along trees, thick bushes and perhaps a fast hunt for the feral beasts of the woods. As I passed along the woodland trail, almost all was dead. I listened to the cries of the distant flee of the distant blackbirds which tunneled through the joust of the softest wind. The crows gathered it's murder and swept from treetop to treetop as the floods of the wild fog and the suspension of the canvas of the sky trembled through the feathers of each.

After walking further, I came upon a well constructed hut, edged deep into the center of the woods. I smelled spiced which would drive men to madness. I listened to the winds smashing across the wind chymed and I heard the sound of speech which most certainly was a woman. I stepped forward and softly tapped upon the heavy oak door and stood silent until a sweetly dressed and tenderly beautiful woman answered the door. I smiled, looked upon her and spoke, "Hello, my name is Young Boy of the Woods."

She responded in a straight shot, "Times are fading and so remains life as we will know and you hold much magic my dear. I am a lady who knows much, yet holds no power or majestical features. The phantom, as I am sure you know, has been destroying the forest and the far reaches of the woods to the desperation of the north."

I said, "Perhaps then, you may know how to defeat this phantom. I have a covenant with the woods. Although an unspoken covenant, a covenant the same. Please fair lady, what do I do?"

She replied, "You must take a mortal heart from a mortal flaxen hued young lady and place it on top of the top cliff, on the top peak and cover it in sage.

Upon great thought, I said, "My Lady, would you donate your heart? I know very few mortals and they are very far from here. I believe this phantom will reach all of the lands spreading glen. You will never remain alone as you would be the spirit of the woods and I will speak with you and keep you dearly within me. Your passage will lead you through the lands that surround; you will be in comfort and softness with the rise of the sun and the fall of the sun."

With a pale face and sweaty hands as I walked her to the shed where the wood splintered, I fed her some of the poisons I found in the cupboards. She drank deeply and in several moments Drifted to a tender place.

Upon the removal of her heart and the pouch filled with sage, I walked to the mountain peak which served terror in the deep hours of night I heard a piercing scream as my blood spread warmed and I shook as a fallen acorns would fall upon the ground.

"Fair Lady of the Woods, please help me. Where is this phantom? Is he near?" I reached to her in a similar dance of the ancestors.

"He lurks behind the tree as sweet fragrances in your pouch make him timid." said The Fair Lady of the Woods.

I tossed her heart by the cherry tree and spread the sage as the deepest, darkest hour of night. I heard a piercing scream as the broad portion of the cliff shattered and fell upon the lower ravine. By morning there was silence and the buds began to grow sweetly upon the tree limbs and bushes threading to the sweeping sky. I hiked on a downward slant and found the tender stream as I drank then bathed in the purring water.

I walked to the cabin, well in the center of the forest and slept for what seemed like an age. As the rise of morning, I spoke with her for months on end.

She Spoke to Me

Once when the moon hung like a hammock, I leaned upon the arms of the oak tree and watched the moonlit leaves flicker in a trembling, shedding coat which flares each dancing leaf, shadows against the earth. The winds crept slowly in a refreshing softness as I captured every spice and aroma as the meadow drapes and passes across me. Gently, I return into the thicket and brush as the fellowship of the woods cloaked me in swabbing cottons and depresses of my leather boots. Further, the moist leaves shrouded me in tears of the gnashing woods. Through the thick heavy branches which moaned with each roaming vines and the crawl of the ivy which spread in bloom and lust, I turned deeper into the wild promises of the wood. Moments past, I came upon the hollow of these cracking trees and softening mint. I watched each layer of bark and the hardened core of the branches which snapped into the inclusion of the marrow of this ancient earth which rose as a haunting chant, the earth and gathered threads of branches upon branches. I haunched beneath a tight row of trees and watched the raindrops gather the sliver of the curved moon as each drop trembled upon the moonlight and the gathering dispersion into the cake of the earth. I spoke to the raindrops which patted upon the canopy on the top slope of the trees;

I asked for food and the trees dropped a sweet harvest of a gathering bundle of nuts.

Smooth, sweet tremble of the maple wood loosened the sap and tender syrup which coated my tongue as the sweetest creams unyielded from the fragrance and paleness of the breasts I once fed and drank into every hour of the trembling night. I recall the sliver and passage which laid way into the cove of bleeding life. Sensibly, I walked upon the heavy rug of the suckling pastures which deepened into the flooding rapture, the minerals which resounds the echo of the slashing twig and the burst of the lime green buds, lined upon the branches and stem.

She paved the landscape of the dark velveteen shroud which softened wedge and nook of the forest and upon re-demption, she sank and flooded the earth with a tender fog which loosened the frigid positioning of each waterbead. There swelled food in her full bosoms and trickling water on her flesh which stood perfect and tangled in her nakedness and I heard the distant roaming conquest from the depths of her lungs. Leaning onto the mosses which spread and shook every motion, it lulled me into the softness and emerald hues as I stepped upon a fracture in the wind which sauntered after me and deflected by the dance of the green upon the bark.

Threads of pink and the slouch of the amber rising upon the round edges of the eastern horizon, I smiled and listened to the blue bird, the robin and the crazed call of the cardinal. I stepped upon the sobbing grass and felt my feet snap the onion sprout and the cushion of the clovers which sang choirs and chants.

I carved my way into the western woods and opened my mouth and lungs to the poise and riveting tastes of perfection. There slouched a silent slow wave of the leaves as they called upon themselves and gripped the slight wind and hosted direction.

The wind slowed to stillness, the trees stood as a sentinel, overlooking the slithering river which tunneled through the forest, field and it's birthplace, the mountain peak which rested in heaviest ice. The sun smashed through the moist clouds and delivered as a prism which tossed a bridge from curved edge to curved edge. As I look to the distant field which stood and waved this tremoring, gathering of wheat; I swam through the memories of her veil and fullness of her light brown hair which pulled me in an invitation. My vision tossed to the west and I heard the gentle slapping of the gathering ponds. I would then recall dipping our soft feet into the tread of the kelp as the sun grew warmer and motioned burgundy flesh across our legs and neck, arms and floods the sky . I stopped and sat upon the soil and listened to the bones of the earth and the rib which stamped as the bringer of all which is life.

"Do not, fear me. You are The Young Boy of the Woods and I recall what you recall. I once loved you as you loved me. You held your nakedness against me as I once held my nakedness upon you. I recall December when you slide your icy fingers across me and I caressed you with warmth. You slept your weary head upon my charms of wheat. The treasure of my body belong to you as every cushion of my groin suckled upon you.

"The next night when the moon curved as a sliver, I became confronted by a dark angel who stood high to the ground and held vibrant red eyes as the wings he wore opened to the fullness of his body length. With the motion of his hand, I flew to the ground as he forced himself upon me and then throttled me into boasts a full hethe soil and clays of the trembling earth. In order to return a dark angel to the fiery pits of Hell, you must call him by his name three times consecutively. If you are able to condemn him to the bowels of Hell, I will be freed from his curse and granted the freedom to be with you upon the curves of the moon and wander the earth in my pleasure.

"One man alone whom has studied this subject for years might know the true name of the dark angel. He lives in a hut which rests on the opposite side of the fields of wheat. The man goes by the name, 'Man by the Field of Wheat'. He stands just shy of six feet tall and boasts a full gathering of pure white hair, rivalling the beds of Winter snow. Upon his body and across his shoulders and into the depths of the high reach of his boots, his red scarlet cloak flutters into the passage of the wind. With a black reach of warm wool pants and the gray rabbit furs which spread warmly across his torso, he carries a purple colored hiking staff and coddles the sweet flavors of his pipe. Please, carve your way through the wheat slouching fields and continue until you find the cabin which floods the sky with ashwood smoke." said the perfect lady with her perfect rhetoric.

I stood quick as the heavens gashed open and moaned upon the trembling wheat. The flickering sunlight daunted and weaved upon my lips. Motioning my body across the heavy walls of thick wheat, I watched as the mice scampered within the deeply rooted tremble of the earth. The sky grew to a sizzle as the warm moisture and humid cascade of throttling day pampered upon me. Dusk began rising across the sinking doubt of the sun and sweet candied pastures lulled me into the safety of the edged station of the woods; from the trembling wheat and the edge of the trembling wheat, I looked with a stab upon the earth.

Looking upon the tall elder man, sitting tremendously still, I revealed myself from the capture of the fields and said, "Hello fine Sir. I am The Young Boy of the Woods and what kind Sir might your name be?"

"I am the Man by the Field of Wheat. I stay here reclusively and seek a depth and thick vein of knowledge. Once I had a companion. She fell to the wrath of the Dark Angel as he feared me and took her to the outer edge of the slapping flames of Hell. Ages have passed as the trembling cruelty swabs across me in the tastes of rendered black blood, softly, I mourn and hold the staff of recollection and purity.

"Perhaps I may have you in my cabin for a cup of tea and a bite to eat. I can tell you've been walking for many days." as the Man of the Field of Wheat extended his courtesy.

After climbing the steps and walking slowly into the cabin, I watched the thousands of papers tremble with the close of the door. Candles where doused and the desks held pages which held languages which no normal man could read. He offered me a soft cushion which deepened well upon the couch. He lit a fire and placed a goblet of wine in the pouch of my palm. Moments later he sat in a large cushioned chair which held him as king of this tremendous home.

"I looked upon him and asked the question straightforward and dashingly to the point.

I opened my mouth with a collage of verbs and nouns, consonants and vowels and said, "I must kill the Dark Angel. He has captured a love of mine and to be in a position to free her I must condemn him to the shattering reaches of the universe. My love sent me here and pointed me in your direction. From what I understand, I must speak his name three times and he will perish."

He stood swift and looked upon me with glazed eyes. Slowly, he pried open his mouth and said, "If I offer you the true name of the Dark Angel, it is I who will perish and I shall roam the earth with our ancestors as we speak to them and moisten with each sweet rainshower from the gushing heavens.

My love has slipped across the deep for ages and tender moaning ribs of the earth will shake and welcome me. If you wish to slay the monster of the depths of the wild realm, ask once more and I will utter forth."

I stood before him and asked again, "Please fine Sir, what is the true name of the Dark Angel?"

He softly stood and said," Charonastics."

I swerved to the door as I heard a tremendous scream which came from the bellow of the Wheat. I grabbed my staff and darted in haste to the stretch of the weaving grains. WIth moments to go, I stumbled upon a rock and felt the paste of the rain which lingered from the recent storm. Now seconds past, I stood before the giant black angel.

"Charonastics...Charonastics...Charonastics," I screamed in a wild pitch as the suckling, decay of the fierce Dark Angel loosened it's flesh and lost each flake of each wing.

I turned as the slow, cool wind taunted it's way upon the back of me and sweetly I cooled and reached the fullness of the tender earth. I stopped upon the wiggling pond and rested my feet in the murky water and spoke to the leaves upon the trees. By nightfall, I rested and slept in these cluttering leaves.

Tenderly she sang to me as the moonlit shadows upon my flesh. I looked once more and drank the coolest water as the winds spoke of triumph and regal prowess.

Woman of the Woods

I awoke under the Autumn blanket, covered with the leaves of the birchwood which I disregarded and stood once the proud winds of fall escorted the leaves into the deeper part of the woods. Having slept for days, I wrestled for breath and slung my cloth and leather boots upon my body as the wind caressed my hair swift into a wild expression of the relic of the woods; sweet scents and flavors burrowed upon me. I shook the October chias I resorted to the friction of speed as I headed to the north woodlands where I last saw her, this moment last year. I can still smell the sandalwood which crawled upon her and shook me to retaliation and treasure which rests upon the shadows of her full creamed breasts. Her eyes wavered the tree branches and projection of light, light which smothers the edges of the intersection of the sky and hosts reds, pinks, apricots and indigo. She opened herself as 'The Mother of the Woods.' Upon hearing the chymes of her laughter which toppled and cast each leaf into a reaching spread of quilt. As I recalled her filled body and the lusty taste upon her tongue; I dashed to the north and breathed every inch a bit more clever. I heard the moans of the ribs of the earth.

In an instant, I felt the tension in my torso and sweat trickling down my temples and moisten the edge of my face and softened my hair. Then all went cold. Cold as the deepest chasm of Winter which coats the soil with ice and fractures the earth with tendencies of the coldest rapture of an early October. I ran with speed behind me as light christened my long shadow which moved farther and deeper into the drapes of the soft woods, far to the south. With certainty, I felt the billow of her sweet lungs as every song of sadness poured from her mouth and tongue as I arrived and witnessed her on the depth of the northern forest which coddled her with plunged blood and the madness of the winds swept across the hollow and chanted the fugue of this fallen night.

Stretched arms and legs, pulled as a 'V', she bore a sharp dagger well into her left breast and punctured the charm of her pounding heart. Trickling blood flowed out the mashed tunnels of her nostrils and plagued drippings upon the crust of her quivering lips. The inner dream of her pale white thighs tamped into the slashes of a sharpened knife; I fell sour to the earth and begged the marrow of my ancestors for help. Black as a velvet cloth, the sky shook with clarity and lay upon The Mother of the Woods as I stood bewildered and knew not what to do. In the fury of the moment, I swiftly climbed the tree and cut her body free of the pain and the torture. I held her in my arms and kissed the stained blood from her as the night grew colder and every posture of light receded to the drafts heading onward and west.

With madness swimming through us, I spoke, "My dear, what has befallen you? Please tell me, who is the villain, your enemy who has defeated you in the month of October? Tell me who screams the plague of guilt and I will defeat the beast. I loved you last fall and cannot let you die alone in the birthplace of these woods. Before you carve your path into the depths of the sweetest marrow of the earth, tell me this monster's name."

I looked upon her as she had but moments to speak.

She said "Brenningston, Devil of the woods." In a swift second, she faded and went searching for her ancestors and all which is antiquated and held in fellowship and love.

With the death of the Woman of the Woods, I hurried to the field of wheat and dashed with the recollection of the library of scrolls in my friend's former home. His name was, 'The Man by the Field of Wheat'. I lost much breath as the air thinned with a rotting triumph of the Woman of the Woods and her defeat. In the section of woods I was in, the birchwood reigned as a sacred tree. I lay upon the trunk and coated myself in the fallen leaves as the swift wind from the north caressed me and cascaded warmth upon me. I dreamed of the moments we spent last year upon this shaking time. Her icy chiseled hands motioned from my lips to the rise of my genitals as the milk of your heavy breasts fed the tongue and mouth of the passage to my quaking belly. The leaves caressed me as I tangled into the slumber of the centered woods. With every nook of every leaf, I swept into the warmth of the straining forest and all the majestic press of a thick tremble and the yawn of her quilts and wool blankets.

Into the youngest age of morning, I dressed and darted across the fields of wheat and ran quickly to the home of the former, Man of the Field of Wheat. He stood tall and strong as an intellectual perfection of a being. Richness in manners and guidance to his fellows which loved and adorned him, he paved the way for the destruction of the supernatural and the wicked. In his final hours, her gave all he had for the destruction of a demon which tortured and devilishly slashed upon all which quietly roamed the ethereal earth.

Brenningstone slithered through the tunnels and gripped me in my ears. I fell to one knee and quivered as the serpent which once reached across the earth. I screamed as a wild beast plunged before the spit upon the lathering flames of adornment which suckled into the boil of the bloods I shroud.

Upon a moment when the wild Devil's apprentice stood tall and and spoke, I heard the words, "I am but inches from you and all I need do is to carve you with the sacred horn of the devil himself. It relishes itself in fear. Just give me a moment and you shall slump in defeat."

With just a moment to spare, I thought of the Woman of the Woods. I held to her fragrance which lofted upon the wind and caressed me in her gifts of prowess and tender governing. She sweetly, secretly spoke into my mind and said, "I will distract the Devil's apprentice and you strike with your blade and remove his horns."

Without losing another second, I witnessed the lightning smash directly behind him and I dashed with great speed and with two swipes the horns fell to the floor and black blood scoured everywhere upon the strengthening wheat and the minerals which burrowed upon the clever soft Earth and the ice receded and the winds and leaves of Autumn returned.

Now, walking upon the blanketed woods which held the growing infant within the abdomen of the farmer's wife, deep in the fresh land where the fields reach ripe and plentiful, she bore a daughter whom will be called the 'Woman of the Woods'.

Evil Sorceress

Once, the rising vapors of Summer, swelled and stung as the fluids from the morning warm droplet of dew, suckled the grass clippings to my boots and swiftly I left the morning rhythms of the sun, dancing upon the treetops and canvas. The winds stepped across the crackling branches and furthered their path to the pine trees which cluttered the needles upon the dressed gown of the cone snapped floor where sweet sap of the wood bloomed in weaving soft flooding winds. Trembling my way across this thicket and thornbush of this section of the woods, I stepped with the lightest feet and weaved and carved through the edging flank where the sweet pastures and the tender miles of meadows trimmed at this start. As the winds cooled, I stepped upon the tall grass and spoke to the nearby hyacinth which coiled in the tender grape aromas. Summer fattened and swelled around me as the slithering winds heightened with the grip of the approaching winds.

Around me, I stepped upon the rise of the yellow and pale green stalks, the wild grasses. Surrounded with the slap of the hot rain, I swam through the crowd of the milkweed and crouched below the shoots of the bamboo. Pausing at the sycamore tree, I breathed the tremble of the dance of the tender air. Looking upon the distant grays which deepened into scattered hues of an endless mesh of charcoals and fleshed ivories along the eastern edge of the visceral flank.

Now, with a slice of the heat and hot slam of the rain, I felt a pause in the mad weather and heard a call, a choir and perhaps a chant from the voice of the ancestors of these curling fields.

"The rain will not cease and the wind will not calm as long as the sorceress remains and eludes as to where she dwells. She tangles with her spells and triumphs with her burrowing magic. I bid you fair warning, she most certainly serves the dark, outer edges of the forest and landscape beyond. My fair, Young Boy of the Woods, you answer to the spectrum and friction of the light of the wild. We wander this earth and collectively smile upon you as you sweeten and polish the reaches and edges of the land you burrow upon and the woodlands you call home. Reach to the lavender bush which floods upon the bank of the cliffs which stand to the peak of the mountain and the mountain pass. Place five petals upon the tip of you your tongue and sit, rest for the duration of the dispersion of the petals. From there you will know where to go and what you must do," said the warm voice of the ancestor.

I replied, "I will do as you bid. There will be answers in this burning heat as the rain boiling upon me and the winds scorch every spot of flesh which remains open to the blisters of this cruel Summer. I serve my people from the past, eons after eons as we pass the proverbial torch, we are the people of the tangle of the woods. Swiftly, I shall purge and remove the fear I swell upon as the beast, demon, devil, witch and wizard, to name a few, I sting the darkness of the depths where the endless serpent slumbers and encases the earth."

As the wind swept and screamed across the madness and heat of the meadow, mountains and forest, I heard, "Swift haste, to the lavender bush and find shelter. Things tend to be worse as the darkness will shroud across the land you covet and proclaim for yourself. At the precise moment of dawn, I shall return to you."

I placed the five petals of the lavender bush gently upon my tongue and I danced upon the spirit of the loving, sweet earth which burrowed the tensions into me and removed them just the same as I lulled into the arms of the reaching syca- more tree. I lay still and cool and silent in the hammock of the strengthened tree. As I trembled into the strong arms of slumber, I looked upon the cliffs which reached the summit of the mountain peak. I could smell the foul stench of the sorceress as the intense heat and wind slouched around and past me. I finally deepened into sleep and waited for the precise moment to awaken.

The ancestor proclaimed at the precision of the moment of the light of morning, "You have found the path to the evil sorceress which harbors hatred in her heart and wishes the most for your defeat and death. Young Boy of the Woods, please let me warn you, if she touches you with the icy edges of her fingers, you will fall to dust and will be blown upon the winds of the Northern Mountain Peak. I see you have the green staff. This will help you in your fury and your thrusting joust of conquest. Aim the cool green light upon the medallion on her neck and she shall perish."

With the sun draping across the crest of my shoulders and the wind pounding at my back, I stood still and looked upon the cliffs which reached the summit peak of the Northern Mountain Reach. The stretch haunched as high as the highest castle. The ivy which trellised down the curving mountainside held a secret. Soon, I could taste the lavender and I snapped in a hurry. The ivy stitched it's way to the top of the darkening peak. I walked and reached the edge where the climb was to begin.

Upon climbing the vines which stuck their way upon the cracks and crossed roots with other vines, I felt my back and shoulders becoming blistered with the sun and the heat of the sun. The wind tossed me between wavering gusts of the tense and heavy tossing stretch of rooted plant. After the wind paused for a moment of brevity, I darted up the vines of ivy and tossed myself upon the sandy and rock laden floor.

I grabbed the green staff and quickly looked around as the sun crept upon the layers of my flesh. I had a sudden icy chill which ran across the spine, rooted in my back. Upon turning around I saw the gnarled, evil sorceress as she came so near to touching my flesh and turning me to powders of dust. I smacked her rotting hands away with the green glow of my stick. In the quick of the moment, I pressed a beam of green light upon her medallion and what followed was a passion of agony as I shook to the sandy earth.

She stumbled back a few steps and continued to scream as the haunch of her body fell across the towering cliff. After a few long minutes, the heavy wind began to slow and the heat kindly subsided.

I gathered my things and walked down the mountain across on the opposite side. WIthin a few days I had reached the luxury of my cabin and trembled within the tenderness of the walls and slept for what seemed like a generously long time.

Great Wizard
of the Northeast

Once I held each staff, yellow and green, in the grip of my hand and I felt no surge, no electric rush, no mystical fezz, I knew there roamed trouble in the meadow, in the forest and in the mountains and edged clifftops. After opening cupboards, pantries, my basement and the fresh foods which stayed snug in the pouches of my backpack, all ready to eat, I felt a loss of magic, or the lack of inherent magic which should flourish along the veins and roots of these tender lands. Upon grabbing the lightweight of the yellow staff, I grabbed my backpack and my cloak and a carafe of dry white wine from the Northern Reach and walked out of the dust and scrapes of the front door where the winds knock onto the face and rusty hinge.

The robust flavors of the shuffling leaves, scraped upon the hard and chaffed dirt, the woodland floor. I gathered this flood of the Autumn breath which wrapped around me and kept upon the crest of my back which glazed along my cloak and mangled the fullness of my hair, a deep chestnut brown. I walked through the rise of the existing forest which boasted and stood proud the upcoming pale green and pale yellow patches of grass and weeds. The grass felt like razors as I waded through the thicket and thorns which scattered their way and carved me far beneath the slicing shoot of the piercing blades of the sun.

Walking through the slopes and trembling surfaces which rise and conveniently fall off making of sliver of a tense and dry valley, I loosened and looked at the half-moon, justice moon which began to darken the net of the fading sky of day. As I approached the Might of the Great Oak Tree, the massive moaning, talking tree could help on the account in which the tree stayed on the rising peak and held no magic. The tree stood as a living creature from the most ancient times of old. It lived as the last of it's kind and held wisdom which none other can compare with, regardless of tender prayer or meditations as they would caress through the forest or sreaming lungs of the mountaintop. Upon the trail, most slender and reaching to the apex of the dancing branches of the trees sign of softness and tenderness, I paused on the smooth ridge of the heaviest of rocks and I sat in dampness and cooling sweats while I watched the rising vessel of the sun.

As the cottons of the soft yellow sun rose across the brim of the earth, I stood and returned upon the path and heard the morning song of the Great Oak and paved my attention to the cracking branches and the fluttering dance of the leaves as they gathered in mounds, moaning to the deepest reaches of the shaking meadow. The skirt of clay, cake and dusty swirling beds of the most slender circle which coddled the trunk and her deepening roots, held a single perched pale yellow leaf; I stopped and smiled upon the song and the might of this oldest of creatures alive and alone on the hillside.

I reached the fullness of my canteen. Opening with the edge of my, I heard the cork pop and I drizzled a few drops upon the dusty tread of the gnarled trunk. Looking upon the surface, I stood and witnessed the rose bush which grew and gathered to the lowest of stretched branches.

"Thank you, Young Boy of the Woods. I have been awaiting your arrival. I smelled your fragrances as the wind soothed in my direction. I softened to the muds and earthly bloods of the soil. With laughter, I listened to your ancestors who craved the press of your feet as the grass and the onion root coil arm and breast. The roses are beautiful. I have myself to thank for that, old roots.

"I listen to the furthest of mountain chains which reach the most northern east and it stems from there in which the magic of our sweet lands dispel and fade as the fog on the brisk stretch from the month of October. I reach every voice and step of every foot. Hearing the saddle of the ice which freezes on the great mountain posture, I speak with the rocks and ancient twigs which ready in a fastening ice bath. Beyond, I quiver to the valley and the screaming rattle of the heavy river which feed this place we call home. I spoke to a wealthy farmer who danced upon the richness of his pastures and meadows with the crisp soaking of nearby earth, alive in every spice," spoke the Great Mighty Oak Tree.

I replied with poise and a deeply fond respect, "Great Oak, where, how is our magic being held? Whom or what is the one to blame for this. I will travel across the width of this great land if I must. Great Mighty Oak, please provide me with direction. I shall keep your words as a secret hidden well within myself and no one will capture it."

"The Great Wizard of the farthest reach of the Northeast lurks in a cottage hidden deeply within the moans and mumbles of the great woods which suckle every posture of the earth. The forest, a pine forest, speaks to the vapors and fog which loft upon the sweet tuck of winds and cool Autumn find the hollow and the cottage will soon appear. Bring your yellow staff. When the light resumes it's magic, you will know you have come near to the wrath and wicked Wizard of the Northern reach," declared the Great Mighty Oak.

"I thank you for your guidance, Mighty Oak. Now, the clouds host the slivers of the warmth of the sun and I will begin this journey with the trembling fog at my feet. The rim of the sky, fat upon the east rises in as a canvas which holds the seeds of the tangerine and purple with a grip upon a trembling sun, I can hear the 'caw' of the blackbird as I take my first step.

As I reached the base of the mountains in the Northeastern reach, I felt the stones, pebbles and rocks as they quivered and shook beneath the grip of my heavy boots. Gingerly, I smelled tasted the petals of these foriegn flowers which perch and grow in the soil of the mountains and the clovers and mint which grow upon the slippery boulders, crack and crevice. Endless rows and standing reaches of the evergreens spoke to the sky and smiled upon me. The earth sweetly called itself as a delicious victory as the ferns danced in a trembling shadow beneath the flickering sun.

I spent a better advance of the year, searching for the hollow. Stretching far past the mountains, the woods spun wildly as the tender, cool breath of the pine suckled upon the weariness I swallowed deeply inside of myself. I grew more tired as this search caroused.

In the dash of a moment, I looked to the warmth rising in my right fist and I saw the staff, alive in a comforting glow. The yellow hush stemmed a softening glow as I felt the nearness of the wicked WIzard, here in the depth of the forest in the Northern reach.

The cottage brimmed with the color of ivory as the birch-wood danced upon the glazes of the crawling ivy and bloom of the hyacinth and all it's heavy purple. I hide beneath the rise and thickness of the biggest of reaching pines. I held the light to the base of the cottage door and unveiled the thickest and most potent magical beam upon the cottage which I could.

I envisioned the old wizard in his cloth and cape. The staff swelled fuller in magic as the cottage shook with terror and smoke. My legs began to shake as the cottage began to fall. Upon hearing a swift scream of terror, I chanted the ancient runes upon the staff. With heavy crackling of the wooden beams I unleashed with a dancing power, the once wealthy pocket of mad fury fell upon the ash of the forest floor.

After an hour of the cottage burning, I smelled the scent of burning flesh and rotting wood. I felt the magic of the lands from which I came, return to the trembling sky and prismatic rain fell upon the sweet flavors of the earth and the forest reached their leaves upon the tap of the maple, elm and slouch of the tall hickory tree.

The two years it took to venture to and from the cottage in the hollow of the woods left me tired but, I felt the cabin I once knew would welcome me with eager bones, wood and furnace which stood as sweet as when I left it. When I reached the warmth of the cabin, I slept for several days as the magic I quested for trembled upon the woods, the meadow, the magical persons upon the reach of every stem and leaf.

Minotaur

Once, I thought I heard her voice, indeed her raspy, sultry exquisite voice, rang true to the silent whimpering of my mind and body which shook calmly beneath the wool of this blanket. These dreams seeped upon the moisture of my lips and crushed the velvets of her soft lips and soft flesh. Sitting up with the slowest motion, I shivered to every thread of wool and every caress of her nails and patient thumbs. I sweetly looked upon her and quivered to the treasures and charms of the softest, most beautiful face as the eyes of her emerald poise trembled through me in dances and the sweetest defeat. Upon reaching the pale powders of her cheeks, neck and rise of her breasts, I could feel the dampness of the cavern which surrounded us; tender caresses of her black, full hair draped across my belly and abdomen. Their spread a softness which bloomed from the sap of her tongue and quietly, I spoke into the quiver of the cabin as the words sank upon her and together we slumped into the coolest sheets, born of silk. Into the well carved, deep slumber which hung loosely upon the rising warm gust of the wind. Upon dreaming of ponds and creeks, I awoke to the lush sweat which deepened upon the both of us. After looking upon the sweet, tense smallness of her body, I slept little and stood. I dressed and walked through the weather which snapped as a howling viper of the Winter bite.

Slithering through these full reaches of the white, mounded branches of the long Winter hour, I walked to the creek in all awareness and wakefulness. Having left sleep behind me, crawling through the bed and it's wools and sheets, I spoke humbly to the bones, deep beneath the carving water. Many years have passed and I can smell and hear the chant of every chip and soft marrow. Tucking my torso and thighs beneath the fold of my legs, I sweetly expelled the verbs from my mouth and from their origin, well into the passage of my lungs. I watched the foams which cast and strewn along the edge of the creek, filled with ancient leaves and driftwood. I watched the brook trout huddle with a gathering of this perfect school. Every endless sound which tampered across every rock, pebble and soft, eager rapid, stirred the motions of my bloods as the snow melted off my neck, head and shoulders. I sat on the stretch of the newly fallen log and relished in the touch of her, the trembling kiss of her painted lips. Her fragrance began to follow me to this wooded sanctuary here by the sweat of the water and through the edges of the creek.

She came, sat beside me and looked into the quiver of the shyness of my shadowed eyes as I haunched so near the great spike of the pine, filled with sap and soft wood. Sowly, gently I turned and looked upon the shape of her perfection and followed the trail of her shadowed breasts which swelled with milks and creams.

"One of my sisters has been captured and murdered by the wicked hand of the great minotaur who lives deep underground, well beneath the earth as the cave plunges. He came to the whitest snow, the frigid icy air and took her for his pleasing. She lived with me as a sister and a Nymph of the Winter Woods. I hear the ancient breath of her roaming spirit which fills me with sorrow. Now, the beast knows where the Nymphs live as soon

I must return. My sisters name, 'Little Creek' will shine to the shatter of the Summer sun and dance upon the worship with the ancestors from which we share. I beg you to renew safety and sanctuary to the realm of the 'Winter Nymphs'. Please defeat the beast however you must. He is vulnerable to magic. If you remove one of the horns, or both, he will perish before you. You must be fast and brave my love. I have never needed a favor as intensely as this one. Please, will you do this for me?" asked the Winter Nymph as she begged in terror.

"You fill me with fear as the trembling ice of Winter reigns and follows upon the longest shadow and their crawl upon the earth. Fear, my love, does not provide the answer, my heart for you and your loving people shake upon the cloak of my trembling shoulders and sweetly I say yes, yes I will attempt to kill the beast, the minotaur.

"Minotaurs travel and hunt by night as the lives of your sisters shall remove by day. We will gather them in the earliest of sunrise and take them here, free to stay in the cabin where I slumber and live. The trek to my home from where the Nymphs lurk and frolic will take three days. We must hurry and use great stealth and balance. The sky will open with light within a few moments. Please gather your things and we will draw upon haste.

I donned my bracelet which makes me vanish and the green staff which holds the charm of change. After grabbing my wools and furs and a canteen of fresh water, I packed my backpack with dried meats and breads. The sun began to rise across the trim of the horizon as the icy pastures spilled out from the woods and I spoke to the ribs and sweet flesh beneath the earth. I washed myself in a sweet blessing.

Well into the spread of the meadow, we felt the softening of the ice which wandered beneath my feet and sulked and formed into the white slopes of every flooding dance of the sun. Watching the crest of the mountain chain stab at the rising clouds in the sky, I swiftly dashed upon the opening trail and made way for the mud and floods on the pathway to the forests where the Nymphs awaited. Upon the softening of the distant warm breath of the sun, I felt an ancient brown blade of grass snap and wilt beneath the step of my boot. I spoke of omens, good omens to the wealth of my family and my distant family. I looked to the sky and witnessed the spread of a golden eagle which tossed a shadow across the cool, wet, earth responding in mounds of glistening snowbeds. A shard of fear, shook and fell from the snow dustings on the edge of my shoulder.

The faun, swift with speed, darted from the early spread of the woods and dashed as the sweet motions of the slicing wind which flooded and slapped across my face. We reached the majestic fullness of the Woods of the Nymphs. I trembled upon the trail and gathered the seven other Nymphs as swiftly as I remained able. Each lovely and perfect to look upon, each carried a scent which burrowed heavy in the bust of me and posted an eager motion upon my aching groin.

"From here you must travel to the cabin in the western edge of the woods. I will return, either as an ancient or as a creature, as I am, a creature of the woods.Please hurry and stay together. Be swift and hurry as much as you find possible. From here, I will place the necklace upon myself and with skill and luck, I shall see you in good time. There rests a yellow staff in the cabin. It belongs to you nymphs as long as you find need for it. Remember to follow the tracks of the walk which took us here. Now, hurry." I spoke with authority and conviction in my voice.

After walking across the deep valley through the high jabbing peaks of the two highest mountain, coated in ice, I could smell the foul odor of the beast as minotaurs have a rancid scent all their own. I remained invisible to all and skillfully kept my footing as I rose to the slight embankment which sat into the base of the rocks and stayed open to the shadows of the flavors of this late Winter evening. I could smell it's breath and as well, I could smell the smoke which slithered out of his mouth. Taking a few gentle steps I could hear a rumbling gasp of furious breath which crooned from his voice as the fire trickled out from the deep corners of the cave. Spread across the curve of a boulder, I looked into the thickness if the deep pouch of the earth and all this wrathful madness. I saw the beast and shook in trembling, terrifying fear.

He stood over eight feet tall and had a massive structure of muscle and held black curving horns upon his head. He had a whip for a tail and had the legs and underbody of a large brown bear. Upon the fur of his breast and abdomen, I could see the dried blood and the carnage of every meal which slipped into the opening of his mouth, filled with razors for teeth. His nose sat, wet and black as he used it to come my way. In a few moments, he stood directly above me and raised his muscular arm and swung.

I fell to the hardness of the stone beneath me and tasted the blood as they slipped and gushed from my now broken jaw. The world spinned around me as the flavors of the petals gathered in my mouth as well did a few teeth. From there, I heard a roar which crushed the edges of the boulders crust which slumbered beneath me. Slowly, gathering my senses, I stood and removed the large hunting knife from my pocket. He moved inches toward me as the girth of his opened arms nearly crushed me to death. I tapped the knife with the green staff and suddenly it became a razor sharp longsword which became invested into his abdomen and with a swift slash again, I removed the left horn which sat upon his head.

The slumped body of the minotaur lay still upon the earth. I searched the cave for Little Creek and sadly, there rested no remains except one feather from her dress which I put safely in the deep of my pocket. I placed the nccklace also in my pocket for safe footing along the trek back to the crowd at my cabin. I felt the sweat groom across the flesh of my body as I continually packed my jaw with snow and ice as I could not rid the taste of blood from my tongue and lips.

The heavy shadows of the scarlet dance of evening opened before me as I smiled upon the mountain stream and softly and carefully, I took a drink and felt the steam rise from my flesh as I whimpered to the Nymphs with shattered teeth and a smashed jaw. A few mornings past, we sat on the reaching turn of my porch and watch the rise of the peach and plum colored sky dance in verbs of peach and soft renewal.

Lady of the Frost

Once, when I traveled to the deep reach of the south which perfectly spread the thickest of woods, carving along to the splash and gush of the often frozen sea. With adornment of the Winter breath which frosted and glazed each tree and limb in ice as the green and brown of the trunk halted into the depths where the roots shattered among the freeze of the once dusty dirt. I stood among the swift travel of the powders and snow. I felt the warmth of the fur lined coat as every patch and portion of skin thickened the blood with a gush and slither of heat which curled my voice into the moan and posture where I felt the trickling melt of the snowy fleece as each drizzling bead soothed and softened. Looking behind the great entrance of the pastures which sulked and suckled upon my feet and fell to the moisture upon the reach and stretch of the buried nakedness of my body, I began to wrestle beneath the most remote angle of the distant sun. I seized the gusty breath of the rise of the red maple and gently we spoke of the approach of death and the retreat of death as the dancing sun retreated upon the lusty curve of the earth. I slept high in the branches as the few remaining leaves swabbed my face in dash of the patterned snow and relieved the cool, burning red of my eager face, eager for the tremble of Spring.

I heard the 'coo' of her lusty, raspy voice which so alive in the pull of temptation swept across the ice of the sea which patiently and softly quivered beneath the edge of the frosted sands. For the past many months, I have been tracking the nakedness of her voice as tenderly, I recall her diamond carved face and the perfection of her form and the loaves of the baskets of her breads. Her voice sifted faint as her whispering words fell as a delicate instrument which lusted and soothed into the harbor of my trickling, trembling abdomen. Leaving the woods and meadows of the malted Winter forest, I searched for the phantom, spirit of her which left the flesh and altar of her whispering triumph and caress of this full perfect body.

Together in the warmth of the weather which fell upon us as the growth of the Summer greens and roots and stalks, we fell upon each others lips and tangled into the furnace of the swelling groins. I could feel miles beneath the earth and soften and polish the ancient bones of our ancestors as the sweeping cold shook me well into the chastity of Winter. After parting paths and quivering to the warmer pouch of sky, well to the north, I slept and lulled through the blend of the seasons as I continually heard the whisper of her whimpering voice as soon I chased the fall of the delicate sun, soothing upon the paleness of her arctic flesh. She would wait upon the edge of the Sea of Darkness and embrace me with the nudity of her flooding wedge where water floods the sands of the sea.

When I spoke her name, I paused directly in the path I walked and felt the the crimson blood suckle upon my veins with the delicacies of my thudding heart. I met her in the precise edge of the heat where the Spring lust met with pale skin and unified between the pauses of our bold touching flesh. This suckled upon us months ago as now she quivered and starved upon the slabs of the January ice. She deepened and sank as she edged near the quiver of her near and closeness to death. As I felt the bite of her trembling course of sanctuary and the passage of her fertile ribs as they blossomed the floor of the forest and arrived with sweet gifts of bone and sweet marrow.

I traveled this seemingly endless trek as the final rite must be held upon the quivering floor of the frozen ocean. I brought her sandalwood, sage and the hair of an ancient demon who sleeps in the deep of the softer earth. The sandalwood soothed her, the sage chased demons and creatures of the dark into the expanse of flight as the hair of a demon swells and blossoms into the magic of the grooming wealth of the earth. Reaching a footing upon the dunes of sand and the enormous slabs of the pure white ice, I stood in stillness and listened to the groans of tender wind which coddled me with the coolest trade of frost and loosened step upon the sands.

I stood in an angular lean against the tower, the reaching pine which cast shadows upon the alabaster cove which hid for the duration of the cloak of the ivory sky. When the trim of the sun sliced through, upon the pine, it stretched it's shadow across the glimmer of each Winter moment. With tense stinging weariness in the hamstrings and calves of my legs, I sweetly sang the song of the passing of our people. The chant rose from the depths of this earth as I could taste the blood which pulled across my tongue and throat. With the gesture of the piercing sting of the sun, I could feel the wrangling fracture of the frosts of the grooming sea. Days later, the limes buds of the twigs and limbs of the forest perched and sang with each popping wave of seed and scurry along the wind. I recalled this moment as each moment swept across the bold seasons, a quiver of the swelling birth. Alive in the floods of the labor of the song of the depths of the sea, I stepped upon the gatherings of her cloak, blouse and feathered pants. I could smell the softness of the flesh of her as each particle and frozen groove, hosted her voice to me as the darkness of the deep sea seasoned it's way to the fathoms of the speaking bones, the quivering spirit which patiently roams the earth.

I paid this visit, pilgrimage, more than a thousand times before she walked her path among the spirits who tremble with her joyously. My bones held strong as the floods of the bank of the cove and sea gingerly spoke my name. With the loss of my tense aching body, I replied in vigor and youth. By daybreak, the sky fell upon me as smoke, fog which dripped through the fragrance of my hair and sweat upon my quivering skin.

I sang the song of the bones we share as they deepen into the sands of the softness of the ocean deep. I cast the sandal-wood, sage and snip of a demon's hair swiftly into the gulping eddies of the wavering sea. The smoke fell upon the scattering, melting ice and in the dashing moment, her ethereal shape, the bust, breasts and torso rose to the edge of the still frosted sand. I looked to the cloak of the traveling sky and witnessed the blanketed sun slowly motion through the haze. With several tears coursing across my cheeks, I felt the blood of the water, creek, stream, pond, lake and heavy crawl of the ocean. In the last seconds of her flesh, I softened every vowel as the sun broke into the expanse of the dome of the sky.

"As you walk beneath the velvet of the midsummer night, each fragment of these ancient bones will flicker across the piercing shards of the mosaic. Sweetly, I shall walk with you, I will hear you and I will sing to you. Your fear lives with your shaking breast and ends with the absence trembling power, alive from the forest and earth of the forest. You know me as, 'The Lady of the Frost'. I know you as ' The Young Boy of the Woods.' Recall how I quiver beneath the warm flesh of your fullness,' spoke the Lady past.

"I helped you appear with the sage and sandalwood and the snip of the demons hair. What do you need to join our ancestors in the realm of spirits?

"I need to offer an item, relic in order to fill this passage, to cast you among the ancients whom love you and wait for you. Time has no real urgency. As I spoke, please tell me, what can I bring to you as the days grow in steady length?" I replied with delicate urgent care.

She spoke, "I need the necklace of an evil witch. If you travel to the furthest hill upon the furthest pasture so deep in the madness of the woods, northwest of here, an evil witch soaks into the ponds which scatter across the forest deep. The necklace will not remove unless you put her into the slippery death upon the dry dirt which flakes in the driest breeze. Please use caution, she remains a creature of much danger."

Several days passed. When the woods northeast of the furthest pasture came within sight, I stopped and called upon a beautiful red fox who darts and prances swift through the forest and stops to perch on the moss and use it's keen eye to spot food and water. I released a call of the woods and knelt gently upon the earth as the sky moaned and drizzled a soft rain, alive in refreshment and cool breezes.

The fox slowly came to me and sat upon the needles of the great pine tree which showered the cones in a sweet scent of reunion with the earth. So near the tree, I smelled the sap and the grip of the bark. Gently, I held my hand to the fox and offered him a piece of dried meat which the red fox took gladly.

"Mr. Red Fox, I need to ask a question of you. There supposedly lives an evil witch somewhere in the deep darkness of these woods. Perhaps, Mr. Fox, you can point me in the right direction?" I asked with kindness and gentleness.

Normally, I mind my own. But that tasty meat warmed me in belly and heart. SHe lives in a hut seven miles north of here. Please be careful, Mr. Meat Giver. She is not one to fool with, she's a bit wicked," said Mr. Red Fox

Seven miles north and I spotted the small wooden hut which sent and carried aromas deep into the surroundings. As I neared the level base of the trembling home, I smelled odors which turned my stomach and made me bend in searing pain. I had with me a razor sharp longsword from long ago. I also carried my yellow staff and quickly seemed to lose my courage. I felt the evil and wickedness as I crouched behind a series of trees.

I used the staff began a fire upon the wooden home. In the blink of an eye, the foul wicked witch stood before me and grimaced and laughed upon me. Red fire swelled in her hands as the flames engulfed the face and torso of my body. After tossing the canteen of water on myself I felt my skin act as a leather band. Swift, I swiped the sword at the neckline of her head and deepened a heavy cut upon her throat. I felt relieved as the blood gushed as a river down the front of her body. She removed a long sharp dagger from her vest and cut the right hand of my right arm off with a slice. I bellowed a scream and fell back as I watched her fall dead to the earth. I raced to the fire and seared the scar upon my right wrist and winced with flickering tears as the gentle rain began.

I took the necklace from her blood filled neck and looked upon it. It held dozens of teeth, different sizes and different animals as the magic sayed deeply within it, alive as an entity alone and by itself. After placing the necklace in my pouch, I nota heavy fireiced a feather which belonged to the Lady of the Frost. Carefully, I went into the hut which raised and writhed in fire and fury. I gripped the feather and made way back to the sea.

The woods stayed pleasant yet, my hand held like a ghost and furious pain stung with every step. A few days passed and I slowly understood, the stump of my pain, swelling in my arm, would eventually subside and the scar would heal.

Upon reaching the sea and cove, I called upon her as she rose to the top of the soothing sea. I tossed the necklace upon her as it dissipated and sank into the brine of the kelp covered water. Slowly, she faded as we talked well into the next season. Quietly alive, I reached the calm and serene cabin of mine as I walked deeply into the middle of the woods.

At the Thatched Hut

Once in the field of tremoring ferns, I trembled to the loafe of the meandering pollens and seeds as they burrowed upon the soft mud which lay scattered and held moisture and promise. Spring carried forth the threads of snows and the loosening fleece which melted in togetherness of the swift blaze of the sun. With the bareness of my leathery feet, I stepped upon each patch of cool grass as the dew droplets gathered my walk into a calmness of temping grooves and depress of the frequent walk of the shadows which remain chill upon the pasture amd meadow. I spoke of the laziness of the slumbering afternoon. Gently, I dreamed of each pink, red, and purple stretch of the posture of nighttime as the needled stars pierced upon the canvas, canopy of darkness. Into the Western woods, I stepped upon the thick, rugged path which welcomed me through the reaching, tall trees and sloping moss; I ventured swift to the Nymph of the Western Woods who pressed her fragrance with every branch and bursting pod. I felt the velvets of the softening earth as the last beam of burgundy faded into the swallow of night.

The woods stretched as an enigma with the blanket of early, eager grass webbing across the edges of the fullness of the lime faded roads. Trees foldled into the earth and humbled in sounds of the oldest of roots. Morning's light rains soothed the quivering leaves and held the soft buds and pods into a bursting exploration of the sky. Well upon the darkest hour of the range of this flooding gesture of night, I walked into the deepest flooded path and I breathed her scents, yet fading with the glaze of the cool wind. After the shadows bent and cloaked upon the twists of path and road, I found the gushing cloaks of spices and aromas blind me into the evenings tremble and the ghosts of the shadow bring me into a lost meld of the heaviest part of the woodlands and hollows. I followed the fragrance of her sweet touching flesh. As the sky sauntered to a thriving quake, I found the grass covered road which led to the sheltered hut of her quilts and carpets gathered across the corners and edges of her home.

Walking closer to the opening of the well balanced hut of the Nymph of the Western Woods, I glanced upon her, spread on her elaborate quilt. Her skin was faded from an ivory pale and held scratched and pealing as each spot of her flesh rose dark reds in wilting patches. She held a necklace of thorns around the soft pelt of her neck which buried into her thick flesh. Her clothing lay shredded and cast around the room as the heavy breasts of her remained cut into slices. Deeply stuck, a sharp carving knife remained buried into the tense grip of her abdomen. I knelt upon the soft blankets above the hard stretch of the earth which felt the tears of the torture which lay before me turn swiftly into the madness of my loosening mind. Reaching into the night darkening sky of this night filled with entropy, I gathered several deep breaths and fell upon the trunk of the red maple as each voice of my ancestors clamored to speak hurriedly and fast. The Lady of the Frost resounded into the writhing tremble of my heart and she gently spoke to me as the perfection I recalled, sulking in the deep of the Winter cove and sea. I slowly, slightly bgan to calm as the tender, lucid voice of her swept across me.

"I see into the deepest reach of the ocean, the soft tremble of the pasture and wild green meadow, and I follow your steps deeply and thick upon the haze of the forest and roaming reach of each towering tree. She lay alone as she has been dead for only a few short hours. You must put her gentle soul to rest as the villian must aquire the defeat which he punished her with being the abdomen, the mortal gash.

"He speaks with images he places in your mind. Being a creature of the shadows of night, he does not have a name. Wearing a velveteen cloak and black pants and a naked torso holding the palest shade of gray, you must track him through these woods as here he claims soverenity of the western woodlands which echoes his faint step. Do not forget the slice of the sword you hold must burrow into the abdomen of his gray flesh. This must be done within the night we bear as come morning he will vanish and transform to a distant being." She softly spoke within him as he slowly took to his feet.

In reply, "Yes Lady of the Frost. I will do whatever it takes to redeem her murder."

First, I emptied a plot of soft grass and soil as the burial ground roamed deep into the earth. Holding her in the cradle of my strengthening arms, I covered her in the brilliant white cloth and a snip of sage which I place in the fullness of her hair. Gently, I placed her soft, light body into the restful quiver of the soil of the woodlands.

I gathered my green staff and the necklace of translucence, invisibility. I carried the longsword, sharp as a razor and I entered the deep of the woods, alive in the shadow. I stepped quickly and used the smells which surrounded me to hunt and track this being through the darkness he finds home. Back in the hut where she lay, I pick up a scent which belonged not of herself. It struck me as the scent of rot and the scent of the deceased.

As I walked swiftly through the endless gardens of the forest, I grabbed a scent which I could not misplace or forget. Crouching upon a thicket and well grown holly bush, I sat in total silence and slowly I placed the gem covered necklace upon me as gingerly and with speed I began to fade. My breath, I slowed as much as I could and concetrated on the wicked odor which fastened nearer and held me to the point of sickness.

In an instance, I saw something like a shadow move from the tree above as the wind hurried with speed and I saw a patch of gray. Twisting myself to the high reach in the tree, I realized the beast doesn't speak and seems to be blind as it held no eyes. He lept from the highest branch of the elm tree and pulled me swiftly to the earth. With all of my force, I kicked the beast in the knee of his left leg. Making a darting turn with the sword, I fiercly stabbed him in the abdomen and fiercly carved my way through him.

Using the green colored staff, I turned his flesh into stone and changed him into a statue which over the years turned to dust and every particle settled upon the earth and threaded vines of ivy.

As the days ventured forward and the image of the Nymph of the Western Woods climbed into each realm of my mind, slowly I heard the pleasant 'coo' of her voice as I travelled west. I would soften upon the dark soils of her grave and sing songs of our ancestors and the perfect voices of our tender peers.

Mortals

Once the wind shifted and crossed the hills and brewed upon the warmth of the southwest, I walked hurriedly to the sauces of the forest, sweet taste and tender pearled droplets hung upon the leaves. The trail which burrowed, brought me to the passions of this thriving court of suckling, the nursing lime colored leaves and the snap of the buds which flood the woodland floor with fertile trembling seeds, I step upon each with minerals and tamping boots. With breathing moisture, the earth softens and moans beneath the soft drizzling fumble of the sky and sinking clouds which reveal their darkened gray stitches as they roam from the edges of the horizon and relax as a canvas in position to feed the earth. Reaching this realm of the crop and dusting woods, I walked and softly wedged near the full ponds, alive in the threading of the kelp, I soothed upon myself in nakedness and the coolest press where films spread and opened. After I removed my body from the heavy soot of the quivering pond, I grew in temptation for the glazes of the falling sky and walked to a further patch of field where the heat postured across me and the grass lay as a carpet. Here in the middle of the morning, I watched the muscle of the tapering trees as they screamed across the dancing smash of the wind. Gathered into the tremor of the nectar of the starving remnants of Winter, the thaw of the earth spoke of tossed ice and sludge to the roots of the shattered month of March.

Having chosen the narrow path which sloped upon the gentle grip of the speech of this softly chewing wind, I stood and quietly remained enthralled at the perfect hue of an emerald embankment. I reached my arms to the fallen clouds of silk traced fog lingered and spread flickering fingers upon the grass covered realm of slumber, filled with an ancient trembling beneath this soft earth of the crumbled bones and sunken marrow into the deep. I breathed an assortment of this antiquity as each gripping moan grabbed me in thriving spirit. My hooked toes deepened into the soft earth as the faintly moist wind sang a wild tune upon the curled waves of my heavy full hair. Standing on this rolling peak, I stood and felt the most warmed of creams as they shook through my veins. Into the silence of the earth, quivering passions suckled my breath which replentished this hill where the dead still moan.

Spring wept upon the spears of the grass as quivering drop of watered pearls shook in the cove of the chalice, alive upon the clover patch. In moments the rain had begun as the fog slipped into the deepened valley and lull beneath me. I felt the rise within me as the edge of my voice shot to the dashing vocals of the wild spinning breeze from above my chanting face and warming bust. As the Spring lust of the carving toes and roots of the near oak tree deepened, I quivered and danced for the rising spirits of the whimpering soils as they burned within my chest. The day slithered past and returned to the choir of the earth. I tangled my sweat to the altar of this mounded hilltop. The stars needled across the velvet breast of the eager chill where the edges of the horizons met where they began. Having been swallowed by the shadow where the slithering voices first awoke upon the tender earth, I fell against the oak and fondled upon the loose clamoring leaves, still layered from last Autumn.

I awoke to the highest pitch of voices which groomed across the wind and took itself directly to the washed sting of my effortless ears. Listening to the screech of the most ancient of languages which resulted in the earliest of times, I heard her beg for assistance.

With the sting of my absent hand and the once broken jaw which slightly shakes in the pressing winds of my beloved Spring, I dashed across the downward crest of the 'Hill of the Ancient Bones', scents of blood filled my nose and clogged into the pouches of my lungs. Spirit of the perfect cheetah filled the muscle of my hamstrings and thighs and I heard in a last shout.

"I call upon you. "Nymph of the Northeastern Reach" is I and I call upon you. I have been slaughtered in the wooden arms of my forest as the birth of the earth will take me in full. Mortals have found their way across the great Northern Barrier and I remain soiled and have left the flesh of my body as now I walk the earth in spirit.

"They seem to wander in groups and hunt all our animals for the taste of flesh. They know fire and do so carelessly. As far as I can relate, there currently roam a dozen and please Young Boy of the Woods, you must save the meadows and woods. Please."

I felt the cheetah, the coyote and the gazelle gushed through the syrups and burn of the blood in my veins. The moonlight glazed across me as the pull of the soil of the earth. As the blood of the slice of her flesh filled the ground beneath her, I felt the tears from the gash of the heaven and the souls of the depths of the roots, trees and swabbing soil pierced there trembling kin upon me. The awakening wind sulked to the ache of my flesh. I began to weaken with the rise of the warmth of the sun.

With a tender stroke of loosened heat, I stumbled forward and collapsed upon the coarse bed of the floor beneath me. With the limp feel of the fullness of my body, I slapped upon the dirt and threaded grasses which tugged me into the old dust which remained within my person.

Now, awakened in the soothing breath of the afternoon breeze which tingled slowly upon me, I awoke to the purr of the forest leaves. After a swift swallow of the crisp glaze of water, I closed my eyes and smelled the remains of once pure blood as it stuck on the woodland floor. Milks and thick pastes and creams loosened and seeped in defeat as the slashes of her body lay as a map of the surrounding woods. With closed eyes, I saw and smelled the fade of the pale pigment of her crumbling shell which eagerly urged to drape across the wind as dust returned her to the sauces and clays of the floor beneath her. In another instance, I saw myself running toward her with the madness of a wild beast.

As I entered this stretch of this realm, I became alert and my senses prowled and hugged each corner and wedge of the earth. Each tree for many leagues spoke softly as each was a cedar tree and tossed the scent through lofting, enticing breath of these fragrant woods. I drew upon the spark of the speeding wind rattled the canopy of the treetops as I slowly came to a seizing halt.

I heard the voice of the cedar trees which gutterally spoke, "She lays on the western most edge of these woods and lays next to the trail headed from the north."

I tossed myself as a jackrabbit and burrowed into the deep of the cedar woods. In an instant, I could see the slithering dirt trail which fumbled it's way from the north.

Holding the limp, cool, chill of her once beautiful, enchanting figure and I swelled in the fashion of trembling teardrops falling from the curling weakness of my body. Wildly, I fell upon the dirt and curled into a crescent moon whose curve of the waist shone upon us in the grace of a cooing female.

"I know not where you roam. I do know how and with whom you roam. The burning sauces in my veins replenish me as I gather you in my slowly strengthening arms. With a most tender whisper upon the caverns of my senses, I hear the chant of our ancestors as I give you back to the earth." I spoke with an honest voice.

"Please, Nymph of the Northeastern Reach, find comfort in these tender, loving beds of soil, deep in these woods which you roamed. Here, with you in my arms I smell the sap of the pine as well as the fragrance of the laughing cedar tree. The wavering ferns blushed across the forest floor and sweetly they welcome you as once you walked with them in quiet solitude. Jade of the spread mosses lay before you as a carpet into a new plateau of this new realm. With this spooling and curling current of the stream, I wash your face, hands and the fading warmth of your breasts as the floating leaf falls beneath the water." I prayed in the bosom of this wealth and softness of the proud, full forest.

Leaving the thick growth of the deep hollow cove of the freshened thirsty forest where her bones will bleed marrow and her rib will soothe the soil upon which I walk; once more, I breathe the spice and aroma from the soft and perfect flesh she adorned. The earth grooved and softened as a quilt which molded beneath my feet. Gingerly walking through the thicket, the rain fell and tapped upon the treetops as each pearl filled me with rejuvenation. It was the last rain of Spring and Summer chanted the hymns of the most ancient prosperity of the polishing depth of this heavy bounty of forests, meadows, hills and mountains.

By midmorning, I found the tracks of the group of mortals. Upon weaving through the softness of the soil, trimmed to a slight fullness, I opened my breath and watched the moisture quiver peculiarly through the air; It seemed to stretch with the wind. The leather boots held upon the stones and branches which scattered through the posture of the trail. Twelve mortals feet tracks deepened across the trail in which I followed. From a distance behind, I smelled the odor of the group which seemed to fill the air in the blushing wind which crossed from the south and trembled to the north. Feeling the pulse of my veins quicken, it seemed an arrival fastened upon me as I felt the twitch of every muscle and the burn of my green staff which held as fluid in my hands. I left the necklace in the cabin which stood far off would be foolish and an admission of defeat to retrieve it and time would not be wise.

I tapped my blade with the glow of the green staff as the sword resumed the shape of a magnificently shaped bow and quiver stuffed with sharp arrows. With a warm green spread across the absence of my hand, I watched as the magical renewal of a temporary hand resumed shape upon the end of my arm. I slouched upon a tall and broad tree which held my cover as the branches were cluttered in clusters of leaves. I breathed steadily and softly with the slowly receding wind. From where I sat, silently in good posture, I could see the large, odd looking mortals camping to the edge of the widening road. Slowly, I removed and arrow from the quiver and placed it in the string of the bow. Sweetly, I let the arrow slice the thick June air and in a swift moment, the largest of the group fell upon the earth as burgundy blood spread across the trail.

Three more arrows dug their way through the denseness of the soon arrival of a heavy rain. Two more men fell upon the earth and quivered in moans and verbs of agony as the wind slashed across the breath of the sky and shook the heavy branches of the trees. I caught sight of the third arrow which embedded in the waist of a woman whom stank of madness; she wore black and gray paint upon her face and held her nakedness as she stood below and looked directly upon me. I held to the crazed branch which fumbled across the burning winds. I had been spotted.

With a wild gust of trembling, massive wind, I fell from the branches of my cover and slammed upon the mud and rocks in the earth beneath me. I felt the bones of my jaw snap out of shape. I screamed in pain as I held the gathering of several broken bones, including a crack upon the top curve of my skull. I felt the mortals as they pounded me with sticks as hard as rocks. I could taste the blood in the cove of my mouth as my tongue quickly became coated. From a distance as I lay upon the earth, I heard the chants of the hymns echo through the moist, warm air. Slowly, I faded as the voices surrounded me in a fasten and gripped me in tenderness and love.

About the Author

Under and within the landscape of nature, Donny Barilla coats the palate of his metaphoric and imagist reach as he uses the tremble of his pen to wrangle upon the fever of his surroundings which flood and weave each page. Donny motions primarily as a poet and uses techniques such as he writes books of short stories and novellas and searches his creativity in multiple arenas fastened through thought provoking paints which slip from word to page to book. Keeping late hours which sometimes bleeds into the rising patterns of the sun, he works in his study keeping an espresso machine close at hand. Here, he allows the softened press of his discipline, awake and aware at each moment. Having placed ninety-four poems in journals and magazines, he also donated twenty three books to libraries, academic and public. Donny took first place in the Adelaide Literary Award for Poetry and has placed on two other occasions. After building a construct of vowels and consonants, the words blend upon the page as he pays due respect to the motions of the English language and passions of poetic touch.

9 781954 351431